Saints Tower

Written by Justin Lamper

ISBN-13: 978-0692389577 (Secret Asylum
Books)

ISBN-10: 0692389571

To my wife, Heidi, whose endless support makes dreams come true.

∞

Chapter 1

A few years from now.

Pristine droplets of rain fell like nails, their attempt at innocence lost on me as they ran softly across the fine oak finishes. A priest dressed in black robes recited hopeful lies, guiding people beyond their grief, but I didn't feel like listening. My focus was on the two holes of darkness slowly devouring the caskets that held everything that ever mattered to me.

I could still hear their laughter on the phone threatening me with a surprise when they got home, smell the sweet scent of the strawberry lotion they always used lingering despite being locked away in boxes. I cherished everything about them, but that was all I could do. I couldn't hold them, tell them I loved them, or even hear them. And on top that, every precious memory of them was already slipping away.

"You're shivering," a voice said sometime later. The cemetery had grown empty, and wisps of fog billowed up like the ground was boiling, but apparently Benjamin Hart had stuck around. He was dressed as serious as he sounded; keeping his tailor-fit black wool suit, bowler hat, and shiny shoes perfectly dry beneath his umbrella. His gristly brown goatee was the only thing he wasn't uptight about. "It won't do you any good standing in the rain like that."

I looked down at my shaking callused hands and then back toward the deserted graveyard. "Convenient place to go, I'd say."

"I know that look, Jared. It's not a safe one, but take your moment. Everyone's entitled to give up every now and then."

"Thanks for your permission," I mumbled. "Still wish I'd pulled that trigger."

"I heard a rumor yesterday," he said a few minutes later. "Is it true that you're going into the tower? "

I felt my teeth clench at the word *tower*. "That *thing* took my family," I said, turning slowly. "I want to know why."

"Your family died in a car accident."

I shook my head. "They *died* because the tower announced their names. It was just like that girl in the precinct had said."

Benjamin shifted awkwardly, holding up a hand. "New York City has always had car accidents, Jared. "Besides, the tower's only been a blessing to this city. Hell, it's been a blessing to the country. Names appear on the door every day, but it doesn't kill them, it helps them."

Growling, I pushed passed Benjamin, marching toward my truck. You didn't see many 1970's Fords in New York City, but there are just some roots you don't leave behind. "Their names were written on the door the day they died, Ben—did it really help them? Kelesa knew there was something wrong with it—I just didn't believe her soon enough. The police won't even look into it."

Ben followed behind me. "You wouldn't have either."

After slamming my door and starting the ignition, Benjamin knocked on the window with his umbrella. If it hadn't been for the rain soaking his suit and the look of desperation on his face I would have sped off.

"No one ever comes back once they've gone in, Reign," he warned as I rolled the window down. "You're not a detective anymore, just leave it be. Go back to work, take a vacation, but don't disappear."

"I've got nothing left," I said. "What if it was your family Ben? What if Lisa and Michael were lying in the ground? What if you saw their names on the tower, and then they were just gone? Wouldn't you at least want to know why?"

Ben gulped, and whispered, "Lisa's name appeared today."

"Then I hope to God I'm wrong," I said, shifting the truck into drive. "Keep them safe, Ben. I didn't."

"The tower is a good thing!" Benjamin shouted desperately as I drove away. "It has to be a good thing."

I wasn't sure how long Benjamin stood in the rain after I drove away, he didn't even hide beneath his umbrella as he stared after me, but it was the first time in twenty five years I'd seen him shaken. Sometimes it was hard to tell whether he cared more for his business partner or his best friend, but he had always loved Kelesa and Kara—he probably missed them as well. The man lived for the finer things in life, and to watch Ben ruin even something as small as a suit meant he was scared. *At least he doubts the tower*, I thought, u*nlike every other sheep in this city.*

I drove through Forest Hill Gardens at least three times before finally deciding to pull into the driveway of the cottage-styled house. Kelesa had wanted something old-fashioned if we ever made it big, a place close to the city where she'd grown up, but also good for raising a family. She'd wanted to grow old here, tucked under windblown dogwood trees while swinging on the porch swing.

Kelesa and I never believed in the tower's so called blessings, but our lives, like everyone else's, had started to improve since it appeared five years ago. The economy recovered, hospitals were reporting shockingly less deaths and sicknesses, and unemployment and homelessness were lower than they'd ever been. Of course the President and Mayor tried to take credit for the improvements, but everyone knew it started when the tower appeared. It was also the time I switched careers from New York's worst detective to security advisor and partner in Ben's company.

Two months ago we'd bought the house.

"Damn it!" I shouted, stepping from the truck and slamming the door. "Damn Saints Tower."

I spun to see a round woman walking behind me, trying to cover the ears of her two children while juggling an enormous umbrella. Teresa Luther lived a few houses down and had welcomed us to the neighborhood the first day we moved in. "That tower's a miracle," she said acidly.

My sigh came out more like a snarl as I glared at her. "Let me guess, if it wasn't for the tower you would have never... had enough food to get that shape."

Mrs. Luther's shocked expression almost made me smile, but that was something I'd failed to do since the accident a week ago. Yes, it was rude. It didn't matter that I'd seen the way she looked down at her children when she'd defended the tower, betraying what she truly thought that murdering thing had given her. It just felt nice to let off some steam, especially on someone that adored Saints Tower.

What would Kelesa think, Jared, I berated myself. *She's not here to keep you in line anymore.* The thought felt like a broken rib. I could feel my eyes watering up so I turned away sighing. "I'm sorry. It's been a rough week—don't really see the reason to be nice— ya know?"

"You're Mrs. Reign's husband aren't you?" the woman said, her tone softening slightly.

I nodded.

"You should be grateful the tower blessed her before she died, she's guaranteed a place in heaven now."

"Oh, for the love of—" I felt myself ready to strangle the woman, but the kids staring up at me stopped me. "Just... just go away. Now!" I demand marching toward the front door.

"Psycho babbling tower worshipper," I grumbled as I stabbed the key in the lock and rammed the door open.

I'd made a bad choice. It wasn't the worst I'd made in the span of my thirty five year life, but it definitely resonated amongst the top ten. The house was uncaringly empty, a twilight zone of silence, and the emptiness felt like ghosts haunted the place. I felt cold, and oddly afraid. It was the same house, the same micro-fiber couch and dining chairs; it had all the familiar pictures and small figurines, but it was agony not have my two angels to welcome me in. I felt a storm swirl in my chest as the house tortured me with the image of Kara, my cute little pigtailed koala bear, running to kiss me on the check as Kelesa's voice whispered, "She's missed you all day." She had been sixteen when she'd died, but I would always see her that way, even if she hadn't grown up here.

Yeah, it was a bad choice. I should have never come back—in fact I should have sold the monster and never set foot in the neighborhood. But it was Kelesa's house, and if there was an afterlife like she believed in... *She'd probably not let me in after treating Mrs. Luther like that,* I thought sadly. I sighed. I'd give anything to see her angry again.

Remember why you came back, I reminded myself, forcing my feet to click along the hardwood floor toward the stairs. *Just get your things and get out. If that tower kills you then you'll have just wasted time thinking of what-ifs, just like Kelesa hated.*

I ran up the flight of stairs, keeping my eyes from taking in all the memories Kelesa had hung up on the walls, but the bedroom stopped me cold. The sheets and pillows where strung across the bed and I remembered the last time I'd seen my wife. She'd lost her metro card, something so simple and mundane. The bed had been her last frantic attempt to make it to her appointment on time. *I should have just let her take the truck*, I growled to myself as I pulled the dresser open. *Then she would have never climbed in that cab.*

I threw my clothes on the bed, found a duffle bag in the closet to carry them in, and started gathering a few essentials. By essentials I didn't mean toothpaste and shampoo, I meant matches, gasoline, and my hunting rifle. I had no idea what was behind those fancy tower doors; the priests said it was ascension or God's domain, some babble like that, but to me it was just as likely a fancy business building. Either way, I wasn't going for diplomacy.

I turned at the bedroom door and took one last look. I should have left, but I dropped the bag and made the bed. I didn't know what it was, but something inside me wanted to prove that my time with Kelesa had made me a better person.

I smashed a picture frame on my way down the stairs. The photo was of us at Disneyland, Kelesa's red hair was matted down after getting off Splash Mountain, and Kara was laughing at her. I had a bit more gray in my beard and hair now, but at least then I was smiling. I folded the picture and walked into the living room.

The room smelt like a bar, remnants of a few nights ago when I was barely coherent. The torture I went through that night still burned inside of me, but I ignored it and grabbed my Glock .45 from the small table next to the recliner and left our home to the rats.

An hour later, I saw it in the distance, standing taller than all the other skyscrapers, shining a brilliant gold and white, and quietly taunting me from the middle of Central Park. Saints Tower's beauty was off the scale, but all I could see was the monster that murdered my family.

Chapter 2

The closest parking space I could find was six blocks away. The crowded streets of Manhattan had been even worse since the towers arrival. I shifted the truck into park, turned off the ignition, and climbed out. As I retrieved my duffle bag from the bed of the truck, I realized for the first time where I was. This was where I'd taken Kelesa for our tenth year anniversary. The Surrey Hotel penthouse suite had been a gift from Ben, but that enchanting night had taken a back seat to the tower's appearance.

I could remember it clearly; chilled strawberry champagne on her lips, a warm summer breeze blowing on the balcony. Kelesa had let her hair down as she danced around like she had when we first met. The tower had seemed amazing at the time—a shining white beacon descending from the starry sky.

A taxi cab honked angrily as I stood in the street, flipping me off as it zipped by, and spraying rain water over my suit. I caught a glimpse off buzzed white hair and a silver stud in his left ear, but he never looked back.

"Screw you!" I shouted, moving toward the sidewalk. Of all the taxi drivers in the city, I run into the one that goes the extra mile to be a douche bag. In fact on the entire walk toward Central Park I only got honked at six times, none of which included crude hand gestures.

Despite the damp weather, Central Park was swarming with New York citizens and tourists, a mix of business men and women, families, skateboarders, and worshippers. The tower was at the center, glowing brightly in the gloom, spreading hope and wishes to those that looked upon it, waiting, I was sure, for another moment to kill. Gothic in design, its square base was nearly a quarter mile wide, four sides stretching to the sky to form an obelisk. Its smooth white marble face was draped by green vines and carved with golden etchings of every language; well one language really, just somehow everyone could read them without translation. The towers scripture as others had declared it, stretched as far as Quran verses, to Beatles songs, causing a scholarly brain fart whenever it was studied.

I approached on the south side, where hundreds of people blanketed in white stood watching as three weddings took place. There were three different priests and priestesses performing the same ceremony despite their different faiths, and the smiles on their faces, I could have sworn, were painted on.

The calm around the tower was at odds with the surrounding city, which made me want to start ranting and raving randomly just to break the annoying hush. I was raised in Tennessee, where back country was life, but after spending nearly two decades in the city this quiet was unnerving. Even when Kelesa had dragged me to mass a few times it was louder than this.

I took my time as I headed North, steering through wedding witnesses and mediators. I'd never really noticed people around the tower before, just the tower itself, but as I watched them I noticed they were all completely normal. Sure, there was a whole

Zen quality to the atmosphere, but people were reverent, kind, and trusting. I'd expected rude, pompous, or preachy for starters—you know the regular religious zealous type which you get excited to see just so you can vent on them by slamming the door.

The macabre sight was enough to get my blood boiling. I'd come here to bring the tower to justice, or at the very least die, but I'd also wanted to lash out at the people who could love the thing that took my family. I had the urge to start kicking the people praying to the freaking thing and then pull out my gun on the others. But no, they had to look all peaceful and happy, just enough that I'd feel bad for ruining their pitiless lives. *Thank you world, thank you for taking away my outlet.*

I refocused my attention on the tower, and ignored Kelesa's voice telling me to calm down. It was me versus it. I'd leave the cult alone, but I would never forget what the tower had done. That thing was evil, and I would prove it.

The west side of the tower was less reverent, less churchy, with a focus toward beauty. The park was decorated magnificently; canopies of white sheltered the elegant ball that was taking place. Beads of rain drizzled off on startling arrangements of flowers, while cello players and violinist serenaded the thousands of visitors. A sign up front read: Saints Tower Ball courtesy of the Mayor of New York City, Forever Free. Five years ago I would have never believed I'd see the word 'free' anywhere within the city.

I walked passed the ball gown and tuxedo rental area, and cut my way through the party toward the north western corner of the tower, ignoring the pleasant greetings and champagne offered to me. It all felt hollow, drowned out, as if all I could hear was the quiet hum of the tower beckoning to me. The tower mocked another memory of a few years ago, dancing with Kelesa, holding her close. I scorned the fact that we'd ever felt safe near it, that we hadn't seen it for what it truly was.

When I saw tears stream down the faces of the people on the north side, I was hopeful. Maybe they'd finally realized that the names on the door they were all watching brought death and tragedy, not hope and blessings. But again the tower backhanded me, knocking me off balance. The tears were of joy.

Describing the doors on the northern face of the tower as grand was an understatement. In all essence of the word the sight was magnificent. Tall and arched, decorated with angles and crafted with a symmetry that seemed too perfect, the doors, for all intents and purposes, looked like the gates to heaven. Untarnished, silver glossy metal framed the edges while at their center each door was imbedded with a round mirror. Currently, the name Ellen Lorani floated like an amber wisp in dooming glass.

Despite the horde of people she wasn't difficult to spot. Bald head, covered in a white handkerchief, she was the one standing in front of an empty wheelchair beaming up at the tower with gratitude.

I'm not wrong, I whispered to no one. *I can't be wrong.*

My confidence rekindled as I marched toward the doors and people began sending hostile looks my way. I'm sure I looked out of place with my black suit, blue duffle, and hunting rifle strapped to my back, but no one moved to stop me until I reached the shallow staircase before the entrance.

Most called them the Wise Ones, but any clergy member, religious leader, or spiritual guide was welcome to take the seven seats in front of the tower, each seat representing one of the seven towers around the world.

"It seems we have another who wishes to traverse the mysteries with Allah," an Arab man in a white hood said peacefully.

"Perhaps he wishes to further understand the teachings of Buddha," the woman next to him said kindly. "Tell us Sir, why do you wish to enter the tower of faith?"

"Just let me in," I said flatly.

"Your weapons will do you no good," the Arab man said. "This tower brings only peace, and acceptance. Violence will simply fade away, like a painter's brush stroke with no dye and only water."

"Have you been inside?" I asked calmly. "Has anyone here been inside?" I added pointedly.

"No one has returned once they have ascended," the woman warned. "The journey is not meant to be known to us in our mortal existence. Even if your journey is met with resistance, the weapons of your mind and spirit will be your only defense."

I smiled impatiently. "Better safe than sorry I say."

A third man stepped up from behind the others. He was dressed in black and his priest collar sat comfortably around his neck. "Don't think you're the first to come here in violence and hate," he said. "It is your folly to have such desires in your heart when you meet your maker. You might be ready to die, but you are not ready to be judged. Turn back now, while your soul still has a chance."

"My soul?" I asked sardonically, sliding my rifle from my shoulder. "It might have had a chance if this tower hadn't killed my family. Kelesa and Kara…they were my chance!" I squared my jaw and darkened my tone. "Now I just don't care. Last chance to let me enter peacefully, priest."

"Do you not see the greatness this tower represents," the Arab man said. "It has united everyone. It has given us hope for each other—it is the symbol of our maker. Mankind's squabbles over what is acceptable, what is right and wrong, they are extinct. The tower accepts everyone, exalts and blesses everyone."

"Accept my wife and daughter," I growled, gripping the rifles stock.

"Let him find the truth for himself," the woman said sadly, stepping aside. "He, like everyone else, has their own lessons to learn."

The Wise Ones parted ways, each stepping deliberately back to make a straight line to the gate. "I'll show you the truth when I get back," I said.

"There's something wrong with this tower. I'm going to prove it."

"Why?" the priest asked. "Why can't faith be enough?"

"Faith is never enough," I said. "At least when it's inconsistent."

I stepped through the assembly of disappointed Wise Ones and stopped within an arm's length of the doors. The door loomed over me like a giant gargoyle, somehow conveying both a gothic and angelic sense, confusing the eye as well as the mind in its design. I felt the nerves kick in. I had no idea what was on the other side. I could simply be consumed or devoured. I could die, be frozen in time, or lost in space. I was scared, but after ten years as a detective I knew how to face fear.

I took one last look behind me, saw all the people who were scared for me despite their faith, and shook my head. Faith was a funny thing. It never did make people comfortable.

When I turned around again I saw that my name had appeared in the mirror on the left. It was written beautifully, reminding me of the times Kara had practiced calligraphy with Kelesa.

I took a deep breath. "I suppose I know which door to open," I said to the Wise Ones as I reached out to push.

The ornate door swung in easily, barely making a whisper of sound as I peered inside. Bright light stung against my eyes as I stepped forward, embracing me in a warm hug as I heard the door closed shut behind me, unfortunately the kind display was not a testament of what I found on the other side.

Chapter 3

Everything was graveyard gray. I'd had few expectations going into the tower, and the one I was sure of was dismissed immediately. I was somehow outside, standing in a field of grass that lay like a frozen river, sapped of life. Phantoms of trees spoke in cracks and creeks that belonged in a Hitchcock movie, and faint hisses and gargles echoed beneath an unnaturally large full moon which cast lurking shadows through a shallow fog that hugged the ground. The place felt sparse, abandoned, and yet I felt oddly comfortable. I recognized Central Park, even in the gloom, and if it wasn't for the dozens of men and women crawling in twisted and unnatural ways, I would have almost felt like I'd slept the day away.

The people, if you could call them that, moved around aimlessly, my eyes following their movements like paparazzi cameras. My seized up heart's first instinct was to cry zombie, but my mind noticed that their clothing and skin looked flawless, like they were ready to visit the set of the late night show. There was absolutely no decay or sickness to the people, and their faces looked completely passive.

They paid me no attention, giving my eyes a moment to peel away from the strange scene just long enough to notice that there were more behind me, and worse yet, Saints Tower had vanished. I'd assumed this was a one way trip, but having it confirmed so quickly was freaking fantastic. *At least I can't turn the coward now*, I told myself. *You'll just have to…* Have to what? I'd never planned beyond entering the tower doors.

Perhaps the zombie people would give me some advice, but I had a sinking feeling that was the wrong direction to be thinking in. The surrounding city was hidden from view, and for all I knew it wasn't even there. After all, I'd ended up standing right where a massive marble structure had been not thirty seconds ago, who knew what else could have vanished.

Standing here like a fence post sounds like a stalwart plan, my brain chided as I slid the hunting rifle off my shoulder.

The unified movement of the people surrounding me was so perfect I felt every hair on my body try to leap off my skin at once. Their gaze, hollow and unforgiving, fell upon me for what felt like an eternity before they let out a gargling primal screech, turning up dirt and grass as they clawed and sprinted their way toward me.

My instinct flipped off the safety and brought the gun to my shoulder before my eyes had time to stop cringing at the noise coming from their throats.

It's odd, the thoughts that pop up when you are about to get stampeded, but I swear when I pulled the trigger my mind was actually wishing they were zombies. They were fast, not supernaturally fast, but quick, like any healthy person set on strangling the dog that had just crapped on the floor. But that was the simplest reason I'd wished they were zombies. Shooting people, hurting them for that matter, was not generally an easy thing to do. As a cop I'd been trained early to ignore the instinct to avoid harm to another individual, but even as the barrel flashed on the pale skin of a normal looking woman, her brunette hair illuminated softly by moonlight, it still felt wrong.

Her head snapped back viciously, the rest of her body following her to the ground a moment later. I turned to fire another shot, barely grazing the shoulder of an overweight man as he tackled me to the ground. It's common for your senses to be in overdrive when in an intense situation, but the cloud of husky cologne seemed strange as the man began to strike at my face.

He managed three blows before another person dragged him off and began gnashing their jaws wildly toward my throat. The ice cold sensation of teeth kissed my throat just as I brought the butt of the gun up and jab the maniac away. The fat man was coming at me again, followed by dozens of more, but I had just enough time to pull my Glock out of my bag and aim it into the crowd.

For just a moment, the migraine inducing screams were silenced by the bark of the pistol as I unloaded the magazine into whatever I saw moving. I slapped in another magazine as soon as the first ran out, but still it took less than thirty seconds for my arsenal to run out. Part of me remembered the Wise Ones saying that weapons would be useless, but I just wished I'd brought more bullets.

It was an odd sensation, to be sitting on my rear end as dozens of crazed lunatics leapt at me. I wasn't really afraid, but at the same time I wasn't going to give up either. As a last resort I pulled out my switchblade knife and began stabbing at the first body to grab a hold of me. It felt like I was going to split in two, and then four pieces, as the monsters began fighting over my body, but for all their zeal the people's pain tolerance seemed small. Each time I stabbed they would let go or cry out in pain, only to be replaced by another person that wanted me for dinner.

I felt legions of pain from where blood was being drawn from either bites or fingernails, but I kept my wrist free as I was mauled to the ground, the moonlit sky blanketed by the bodies atop me.

I could barely move when the screaming stopped, and the zombie pile began scrambling to get off me, occasionally lashing at each other as they stood and backed away.

"That all you got?" I mumbled incoherently, still stabbing wildly even though my knife had disappeared. I felt myself laugh at my luck, but cringed at the pain in my ribs.

"Why are you hurting them?" a soft female voice asked outraged.

The woman that stepped from the group of lunatics was quite beautiful. Her Hispanic heritage was strong; long black hair fell below her flawless sun kissed shoulders, but the out of place blue eyes were her most alluring feature. Her face from the nose down was covered by a thin black veil that matched a lacey black shirt that lapped gently in the wind like waves on a beach. Usually I didn't notice people's shoes, but she wore high heels. High heels that nearly pierced my jugular as she used her right foot to pincer my neck to the ground.

"Why are you hurting them?!" She demanded again, a dangerous fire growing behind her eyes.

"To stop them from eating me alive," I mumbled through a gargle of blood. I could instantly tell that my answer met deaf ears so I added, "What's it to you?"

I expected to see rage fill those blue eyes, but instead I saw a sad understanding. "You're one of them. But why would you bring weapons?"

"One of who?"

"An outsider—a fool. You have come seeking answers within the tower's walls instead of believing. You will not find them here. Unlike the others, you have failed before you even began. Now, be on your way vagrant."

The pressure on my throat vanished as she stepped away to comfort one of the lunatics. "It's alright," she whispered. "The danger has past. Remember what we talked about before? Use this moment of courage to think upon your sorrow, let your fear give you focus. You mustn't stay bound here forever."

The simple act of me struggling into a sitting position elicited another unified vision snap from the crowd, but this time they settled down after the woman in black gave me an 'are you serious?' gaze. My eyes darted around for any sign of my knife, but all I could see were pacified people, all listening dolefully to the woman's soothing words. Her tone reminded me of the sweet way Kelesa would talk to

Kara when she'd been a toddler and had spilled water on the laptop. Kara knew she'd done something wrong, but Kelesa had to point out exactly what. She was treating these wild grown adults just like naïve children. "Take your time. I know it isn't easy, but like always, the choice is yours."

"Hey lady," I groaned, "I don't mean to interrupt, but if I stand up are these...*things* going to attack me again?"

She stopped her soothing long enough to lock eyes with me again. "They will restrain themselves whilst I am around, now be gone."

"Where do I go?" I asked. "You said I was in the tower? Then who's in charge?"

"Your questions are not for me to answer. Besides, like I said, you have already left yourself with no means of leaving."

I pushed myself off the ground and grabbed my bag. "You mean I'm stuck?" I shook my head. "I can't accept that. Listen here, my wife and kid were killed because of this tower; I'll do whatever it takes to find out why."

The woman whirled on me, and it was the first time I realized how tall she was. Despite only matching my six feet in her heels, it felt like she was looming over me as she glared. "The path is barred to you. Even I cannot help you move on. Please allow me to return to my work."

"Why am I barred?" I asked.

"Because you have taken away another's chance at finding the door." She looked around at the dead corpses around us. "You have taken away eleven chances. You are damned."

"That's just a bunch of crap," I said angrily as I took in the gruesome sight of the people I'd defended myself against. "They attacked me. What if they had killed me? Would they have been damned?"

"Yes," she said simply. "One's chance to find the door does not last forever, so do not tempt them any further."

I finally spotted my knife about five feet away, sticking up from the chest of one of the lunatics. "You're blaming me?" *This is getting nowhere*, I thought. "Say I wasn't 'damned'" I said taking a careful step toward my knife. "How would I find the door?"

The woman's smile was placating. "You would listen to the voices, follow the whispers, and understand why you are here. Then the guardian would let you pass."

"Sounds like a fairy tale," I grunted, grabbing the knife by the hilt and yanking it out of the corpse.

"Far from it, Jared. It is a struggle, and as we all know, true answers require a struggle." I shivered at the sound of my name, her words seeming to bring an odd glint of desire into her expression—as if she got off on the idea of people's misery.

I was about to ask how she knew my name, but she turned to walk away, her slow stride somewhat serine, carefully masking a deep sensual nature. It took every bit of my focus not to follow her, but as if they were a flock of sheep, the lunatics followed after her desperately; some crawling, others walking, but thankfully all leaving me alive.

Eventually the moonlight drowned out their features until they were just silhouettes beneath the gnarled trees. I was left alone, and the night suddenly felt very cold. The teeth marks in my arm pulsed with irritation, reminding me that I'd just been attacked and should get moving. I kicked something hard as I started walking, and bent down to pick up my empty Glock. I put the gun in my bag, but carried the knife in front of me. I would have been upset about how shaky I was, but considering I was almost killed I let it slide.

I kept my body small as I moved across the forbidding lawn, the occasional distant moan showering me with doubt that I would survive another attack. My breathing was heavy as I jarred to random stops at the slightest noise—where was I? From the moonlight reflecting off the lake to the north I figured I was somewhere in the lower loop of the park, but that didn't help much. This place, this thing, or whatever the tower was, clearly wasn't what a building. The woman in black hadn't given me much to go on except that I was 'in the tower', whatever that meant. I only knew one thing, and that was that I wouldn't accept my supposed damnation without a fight—this place might still hold answers.

I was out of my element. As a former detective logic was usually my favorite ally, a tool that derived answers from evidence and deductions, but in this place even common sense felt foreign. My body shook from the irrationality of where I was, inside a tower with no inside, or it might be rabies being bite by lunatics.

When the first street came into view I hid in the shadows. I didn't see anything, but the empty, vehicle forsaken gap felt dangerous. Empty buildings stood quietly with their doors either barred shut or hanging from their hinges. The absence of car horns, police whistles, and the normal parade of footsteps told me that despite its appearance, this was not Manhattan.

I tensed as a man darted out of the trees and crawled onto the street. His business suit was pristine, probably costing in the thousands, but he almost looked feral as he looked left and right as if seeing some kind of invisible traffic. And then, just like a normal person he stood up, walked casually to the other side, and entered a jewelry store. Again, logic decided to crumble, leaving me standing there with my mouth half open.

It took several minutes to regain control of my mind before I risked stepping onto the vulnerable street. Making certain to avoid the jewelry store, I walked just as the other man had and made it across safely. I quickly dropped into the shadows of the first building I touched, hiding from the sensation that eyes were following me.

I looked back at central park, proving to myself that the tower really wasn't there. I wanted others to see the tower for what it really was, to expose it and bring it down for killing my family, but I couldn't do that if I couldn't escape. Worst of all I had no way of proving any of this was even real, no one would believe this, I still wasn't sure I did. I wanted someone to blame! I needed to understand why I'd lost my wife and daughter, when instead the tower should have helped them, just like everyone else. At that moment I'd wished the lunatics had just killed me. I couldn't handle their loss; the turmoil in my heart was too much. The idea of beating the tower, of uncovering the truth, had tempered the pain, but now... now I just had nothing.

The closest thing I'd seen to a real person was the woman in black. *Maybe she was responsible*, I thought desperately. *I should just go back and take her out.*

I slammed my fist against the wall, knowing that wouldn't work. I sucked on my bleeding knuckles and shook my head. I'd already made mistakes like that before, I couldn't just make assumptions. I'd promised myself I wouldn't do it again.

I told you Jared, you are a good man, I heard Kelesa's voice say. *Your past is only your enemy if you didn't learn from it.*

"Well, what if I haven't Kelesa?" I whispered back as I leaned my head against the wall. *That woman knew more than she was telling me. I was a terrible detective, but I know what it looks like when people are holding back the truth.* I took a deep breath trying to push away the other part of what the woman had said. If she was right I'd just killed eleven more innocent people, and stopped them from finding a magical door.

The door—I supposed that was something; maybe a clue toward understanding the tower. It wasn't much, a single door amongst thousands of doors, but the idea got me to my feet. I came to take down this tower, or more importantly find out why it killed Kelesa and Kara; hopefully I still had a chance.

Chapter 4

I made it three blocks before they started chasing me again. They moved more like hellhounds than humans, tearing after me in what could only be explained as bloodlust. I could feel the cuts on my arms and legs reopen as I pushed to stay ahead of the mob, my heartbeat thumping a mile a second.

It had started out as one, a lone young man in his twenties dancing in the street, and then I'd kicked the can. The racket it made sounded like a nuclear bomb, and then he was after me. The more I ran the more joined in the chase, each behaving like your classic deranged old man after setting foot on his lawn.

I was just about out of time when I turned down a dark alley way and saw my life line. A rickety fire escape hung loosely a dozen feet away and I wasted no time reaching it. The ladder threatened to feed me to the mob, but it lasted long enough to get me to the second story. I took no chances, kicking the ladder away from its rusted hold, sending it down on top of the head of the lunatic first in line for the Jared Reign special.

I stomped on a few fingers and started climbing the tiny stairs to the next story, but when I looked back the group was dispersing as if the credits to a movie had appeared. The anger, rage, all of it had simply evaporated.

Lunatics, I mumbled in an effort to slow my breathing.

My eyes felt like stones as they took in my surroundings. The blood loss wasn't much, but I was ready to fall over from exhaustion. The edges of my vision were getting darker and I needed a place to crash; someplace warm or I'd freeze to death. I had matches in my bag, but I wasn't exactly in a forest, and the few flammable materials were likely back on the ground.

My eyes landed on the window just above me and I moved closer to see if it was unlocked. If I could only get inside I would probably be able to make it until morning. My hand fumbled for leverage as I peered in the window. I gasped as two pale white faces sent me reeling back enough that I nearly tore the fire escape from its mounts. The two women were locked in a trance of morbid hunger. They stared at me through the thin sheet of glass like Chinese food had just been delivered.

I moved slowly, but my decision was quick and likely stupid. I jumped through the hole where the ladder had been severed and started down the street again, and that's when shock started to take over.

All I could think about was how many lunatics were sitting inside that building, how many were just waiting for me to make the slightest noise. I didn't even pay attention to where I was walking anymore. I had my hands wrapped around me for warmth and my eyes were on the ground, scanning for any stray pop cans. The night was too quiet, my careful footfalls the loudest sound in the city.

I figured I'd wandered for probably twenty minutes when I saw hope. At first I'd shrugged it off as a mirage, I was familiar with shock, figuring I was just getting to the delusional stage, but the bonfire called to me.

I pulled out my knife again and slowly moved toward the welcoming warmth. Obviously someone had lit it. Knowing my luck today, the lunatics probably used fire as bait. The beckon of light was in a shop, but the flames ruined my night vision enough that I couldn't make out the sign above the door— something about clouds. All the windows save one were broken, replaced by makeshift boards and pieces of metal. Unfortunately the flames blocked the good window so I had to chance the door blindly.

I could feel my limbs began a little celebration at the thought of warmth as the handle gave way and I pushed the door open. The heat of the room engulfed my frozen body immediately, but as soon I my eyes adjusted I heard a distinct click behind my head.

"You have two seconds to say something or I'll blow your head into pieces."

My brain felt like it had to run a marathon before it finally came up with something. "Hi," I said.

"That was three seconds."

The red hot rush of pain in my head only took a moment to transform into a pillowed darkness.

Chapter 5

The first thing I was aware of was a summers sunset dancing on my eyelids. The oranges and reds made me wince as the pain in my skull laughed at me. The smell of fire and the touch of boiling sweat running down my forehead eventually encouraged my body to roll over, forcing my head to hit something rough.

My eyes shot open to see a man's boot idly tapping against a double barrel shotgun. My attacker, I assumed, was sitting on a wooden stool staring down at me through famished brown eyes. His splotchy unkempt beard was specked with grey, and he looked like he was wearing junk pulled from a garbage bin. His face was gaunt and looked too young for the grey. He was probably in his early forties, and I'd had nightmares about the look he was giving me. That familiar loathing respect brought back a swirl of memories.

The papers strewn out on the metal table were horrific; their predominate feature being the severed left arm and eye. There were nine women in total, each being found in their homes in lower Manhattan, each twisting at my stomach with guilt. They all came back to this kid. He was calm, arrogant, his tongue playing curiously at the blood that trickled from his bottom left lip from where I'd thrown him against the wall. He hadn't gotten far, nearly getting himself shot during his mad dash through the city, but he had stabbed two officers.

"Herse?" I mumbled coming back to the present. "What are you doing here?"

He seemed to snap back to the present as well and frowned down at me. "Well Detective, after I was released from prison I got myself trapped in this cesspit. Apparently the tower just doesn't sit well with people like us, does it?"

"What do you mean?"

"You know, killers, murderers, however you want to put it. Come on; pull yourself off the ground—you look like a worm."

Still a bit woozy I managed to stand, never taking my eye off the serial killer and his shotgun. It had been sixteen years since I'd last seen him. At least then we'd had bars between us.

"I couldn't believe it," Herse said, as he checked to make sure the gun was loaded. "Makes a sick kind of irony I supposed. The first non-viper I've seen since Sid is you."

"Viper?" I asked, wiping a blanket of sweat from my forehead.

"Yeah, vipers. That's what I call the people here—you know because they snap at any sound. Wham they're comin' at ya, savage as can be."

"Surprised you didn't kill me while I was out," I said, examining the room for an escape. It was a pawn shop, a bit dusty with a ma and pop feel, but at the same time it took no effort to hide the fact that it sold a variety of firearms.

"Didn't you hear?" Herse said proudly. "I'm reformed. The world's gone all Zen. Heck they even dropped my life sentence to time served two years ago. Killing you would have messed that up. Besides, you're not my type. I like red heads." He flashed a smug grin. "Ah but I forget, so do you. How is Kelesa now days?"

"Dead," I growled.

Victor frowned. "That's a shame—she had lovely eyes." He paused considering. "You know, I really have to thank you."

"For what?"

"Catching me of course. It really changed my life around, cleaned up my act."

"Right," I laughed sardonically. "I didn't think serial killers could clean up their act. Unless you mean, you've gotten better at killing innocents."

Herse leaned back in his chair and stroked his beard. "Oh, I'm sure I'm better, but that's beside the point. When they first passed the Redemption act, you know one of those everyone's got rights woohaw, I admit the first thing I did was try to find another young girl to help embrace life."

"Sick way of putting it, but go on."

"Hey now, just because we don't see eye to eye don't mean we can't respect each other. We both grew up in Tennessee after all, it's who we are. Anyway, after collecting a potential list of worthy candidates, I decided on this sweet southern honey that'd just moved to the city for an internship at an advertising company. The problem was that about two weeks into my courting process she told me she knew who I was. The messed up part was she didn't care."

"So what? Did it take all the fun out of it?" I said disgusted.

"Fun isn't the right word, but yeah. There was no meaning behind it anymore." Herse stood up suddenly, looking out the window. "Felt as empty as this place."

"So you're done killing then?"

"What? Oh, I might be. The girl I picked after that didn't react that way when I told her who I was, so it wasn't always that way, but that one girl was like kryptonite. Amber. The very thought of her just scrambled my brain whenever I helped others embrace life."

"How'd you end up here then?" I asked, trying to see what he was looking at. The window looked solid black in contrast to the fire, but he seemed intent on something.

"Amber's name appeared on the tower. She'd inherited some kind of fortune from a distant cousin a few days later. Most people would have lived a happy life with that money, but she decided to donate it all to charity. Three days later she was found dead in her apartment complex's pool." He sighed and looked back at me. That arrogance I'd seen so long ago was no longer there. "This tower has the world wrapped around its finger. I won't pretend like there is something right about this place when it goes and kills people like her. I'm here to take it down."

I looked at Herse incredulously, unable ignore the hypocrisy of his words, but at the same time unable to doubt the truth I felt in what he said. Victor Herse was a serial killer of the worst kind. Behavioral analysts had an impossible time figuring him out. His views on life and death were ambiguous. Most figured embracing life meant you didn't truly appreciate it until you were dead, but Herse always acted as if his victims were still living afterward. He'd live in the victim's apartment, eat at their favorite restaurants, buy their friends flowers, and take care of their pets. He was smart about it to, using texts and voice recordings so that people never knew that the young girl had been killed until he was ready to move on. Finger prints and DNA samples should have been simple if he was close to the victim's body for so long, but he was meticulous at crime scene clean up. He'd only been caught when his trophies were discovered after a rain storm had forced a homeless couple to break into his house. After we knew what he looked like we found him casually attending the book club of his last victim. My best guess on why, was so that he could understand why they hadn't appreciated life.

Herse's mind was a scary place; just seeing him again had me second guessing naming the vipers lunatics. Yet, here I was agreeing with him about the tower, barely caring that this serial killer had been set free. This man had threatened Kelesa's life after being sentenced, but the tower was what had actually taken it.

"We have a visitor," Herse whispered. "I never thought I'd see her again."

Herse opened the front door and stepped out into the night. I took the opportunity to look around the shop for a weapon. I scrambled to find the right ammo for my Glock, but Herse was already stepping back into the shop when I found it.

"Grab the crossbow," Herse said as he scratched at his beard. "I wanna show you something. The crossbow will attract less attention if we need it."

I probably looked like a deer caught in headlights, but shrugged it off, finished loading the gun, and grabbed the crossbow.

When I stepped outside Herse had his finger to his lips while his other hand motioned for me to stand next to him. Fifty yards away the woman in black was gathering a group of vipers. She was talking, but it was hard to make out what she was saying. Herse's forearm hit my chest hard.

He looked at me carefully before lowering his arm, and it was the first time I noticed that I'd walked forward.

"Creepy, aye," Herse whispered. "The vipers flock to the siren like she's their messiah or something. I can feel her calling me to, but we gotta ignore it, keep our whits up or we'll be just like them."

"What do you know about this place?" I asked. "How long have you been here?"

"I've been here about three weeks."

I took a skeptical look at Herse's sunken face. "I don't need years of detective experience to know that's a lie."

"Twenty days," Herse said confidently, his dark eyes turning on me. "This place doesn't sit right with anyone for long."

"You look ten years older than I do."

"Yeah, well that happens," he said annoyed. "I might be off by a few days, since it's hard to keep track with no sunlight, but Sid was only here fifteen days and he looked over seventy. I'd say I'm doing just fine."

"Who's Sid?"

"Sid was the guy that saved my life after I almost gutted myself running from the vipers. He basically ran Cloud Nine pawn shop, after a young girl had showed him that fire was a good viper repellent. Seems we just rotate through the shop until the next sucker comes along and takes over."

Herse nodded his head toward the crowd of vipers. "Sid's over there, toward the front, second from the left."

My eyes followed Victor's towards a middle aged man that reminded me of my freshman college professor. He was clean shaven, hair combed over to hang from one side of his face, and he wore a suit that look like mine, only un-torn and unstained.

I wanted to tell Herse he was crazy, that man wasn't anywhere near seventy, but there was no point in beating a dead horse so I just said, "He looks fine to me."

Herse rolled his eyes. "Of course he does, all the vipers look like their ready for Sunday supper. It's the reason I keep my beard, reminds me that I'm not one of them yet. I'm tellin' ya, Detective, this place saps your life until your mind breaks, and then you become one of them." Herse sighed as he looked at his old friend. "He was fine when I meet him, but then one day he started seeing blood everywhere—on the walls, the door handle, on me. It was all in his head of course, but it only got worse from there. Then I woke up one day and he was giving himself a bath and shaving. He'd warned me, kinda like I'm warning you now, but it still got him, and I still almost let him rip my throat out."

I felt my eyes drift back to the woman in black. In my mind's eye I saw a brief glimpse of me kneeling there at her feet, feeding off of her words, desperate to find some sense of peace or mercy in them, and then snapping and killing the first person that came by when she was gone. It felt nuts to be taking Herse at his word, but the idea of becoming one of them terrified me. If I truly was stuck here like the siren had said, and that was my fate, I needed to move fast.

"Do you know where the door is?" I asked Herse when we stepped back inside. The woman in black had departed, leaving the vipers free to berserk at a moment's notice.

"We ain't gonna find it," Herse said gloomily. "If you're standing here that means you fought your way here. Even Sid admitted that the siren was truthful when she called us the damned." A big smile came across Herse's face. "Say, I can't blame you for knocking out a few vipers, they're savage beasts after all, but when I saw you on the news—"

"Shut it," I muttered quickly. "If you can't find the door what's the point in waiting to become one of them?"

He walked over to a rocking chair and sat down, kicking his feet up on the glass counter. "Oh, I dunno. I kinda like it here. Keep the fire burning, scrounge for food, sleep under the desk—nice comfortable routine."

"You can't be—"

"Of course I'm not serious. I've been waiting for someone like you."

"What do you mean?"

"We'll there's a few of us normal's left, but not that many. So, when Sid flipped, well our plan kind of... fell apart. I've tried to convince the others, but they are either cowards, cowards, or cowards. Some are scared, others won't kill another viper, but I know you ain't a coward. I even think we can set aside our differences and work together. That door is my only chance to meet whomever this tower belongs to, and your only way to do whatever it is you're here to do."

I didn't want to openly state that I was considering working with this...loathsome creature. In my mind he was worse than the vipers, but I didn't see another option. So, I decided to at least hear what he had devised. "I want to know why this tower killed Kelesa and my daughter."

"This thing got Kelesa too? Well ain't that just..." His face was actually turning red with fury. "This thing's got to go, Reign. It has to go now."

"Taking all your targets, is it?" I said coldly.

He glared at me murderously without moving for over a minute. "I won't pretend like I understand you, just give me the same courtesy. Let's just get through this, shall we?"

"What's the plan?" I said dryly, my tolerance for being in the same room with Victor Herse hitting the bottom of the bucket.

"We'll I'll make it real simple for you," he said sitting up straight. "We kidnap one of the new visitors before they can make the same mistake we did. Then if what the Siren said is true, we wait for them to lead us to the door, and take whatever opportunity comes up."

"How often does someone new arrive?" I asked, nursing the idea. It wasn't solid by any means, my limited knowledge of anything within the tower possibly setting our course towards disastrous, but it was all I had to go on.

"That's one of the problems—you're the first one to show up in ten days."

Chapter 6

It took thirteen. Thirteen days of sharing a room with a serial killer.

I stared at myself in the mirror, my mind trying to rememorize the new lines on my face. My checks were sunken, and my skin was stained white with ash from the fire. Kelesa used to enjoy running her fingers through my thick black hair, but now it was stringy, and a faded brown. I looked like a decrepit ghost. I still had on my suit, but it had decayed to the point of slum wear. Finding a replacement had proved impossible, since the vipers seemed to covet clothing more than anything else in the city, often ripping each other to shreds for a hat.

Victor on the other hand hadn't changed much physically, but mentally… It was a feat of tolerance to sleep next to him in the first place, but now each night—night being relative—it was something obscene. His rambling had started on the third day, small incoherent words, but by the sixth he was reciting vivid memories in a manner that crossed the line of sanity. It was like the memories were hurting him, torturing him to the point where every thought added one more hot coal to his back. I'd thought last night was the end when I saw the knife in his hand, trembling near his chin, but then he just did what he did everyday; reasserted pressure on me to shoot him if he ever shaved his beard and became one of the snakes, then he would just go back to tinkering with things around the shop.

Thirteen days seemed an eternity to wait for a chance to escape this tower, but we didn't squabble it away. For one I'd gotten better at using the crossbow; the silence of the weapon proving invaluable while moving between the shop and the park. The vipers, however neat and tidy they appeared, tended to be sporadic when it came to their day to day business. They would fancy themselves up and then roam randomly, almost blindly, ignoring everything except for Victor and I. They never ate or spoke, and when they went to the bathroom they just went. It made for a few setbacks and injuries, but each day we were able to add a little more flare to our plan.

I'd picked a spot near the lake for my daily stakeouts. It was near the base of a large dogwood tree surrounded by dead rose bushes. It provided some cover, enough to hide behind while still having a clear view of where I had entered the tower; most importantly the wind rushing through the tree branches masked any sound I naturally made while shifting positions.

I belly crawled the last few feet to my spot, slipping off my duffle bag carefully. Central park was packed with vipers, oddly popular considering the vast amounts of seemingly empty streets surrounding it. It took nearly an hour to move from the street to my spot without alerting the vipers, and by then my feet were freezing. Moving barefoot on cement or asphalt was great for stealth, but it came with a price.

I took a careful look to see if there were any straying vipers looming my way and then pulled the rock from my foot. I was careful, merely clenching my teeth instead of screaming. I seriously regretted rushing into the tower in my funeral clothes. If I'd known what I did now I would have come in full tactical gear. But at least I had shoes and socks, which I pulled out and put on like they were a warm blanket.

As I pulled out an unwrapped power bar, lifted from one of the abandoned markets, ghastly wails blared in the distance, echoing off the skyscrapers. There were others like me and Victor here, hiding in other parts of the city. I'd never met any of them, but it wasn't hard to tell when the vipers got a hold of one.

I scanned the field for any reaction, but the vipers never moved from their dreamlike state.

Sleep was pulling me down. It was impossible to get enough while in the tower, but this was something different. It was a fight to keep thinking sometimes. It reminded me of the first few days after losing Kelesa and Kara. I'd barely moved from my truck, pushing the limits of starvation, only stopping for gas so I could drive past the tower twenty more times.

Keeping my eyes open was a challenge, and my mind hated me for it. I spent too much time thinking under this tree; memories better left forgotten seeming clearer while the recollections of my family eluded me. My passion for bringing down the tower was losing its fire. I was miserable. I just wanted to shut off, and it seemed that's exactly what this place wanted me to do. All I had to do was push that button and I would—

A voice came from the center of the field and I sat up, realizing for the first time I'd been laying on my back.

"Hello?" the voice asked. "What is this—"

The freakish human screams were so close this time that my hands instinctive covered my ears, and all I could do was watch as the vipers snapped awake and tore through the field toward the towers next victim. The moon fell on the man's face as he was thrown backward onto the ground. The utter terror painting his features as he was pulled under the onslaught tempted my whole being to flee, but I held perfectly still, letting the shock take control instead. The sound of broken bones and tearing flesh twisted my stomach, and I had to fight to swallow the vomit down for fear of attracting the same attention.

The wailing stopped a few minutes later, the bloody faces of the vipers reappearing as they were finished with the man. The viper's didn't even look around when they were done, instantly resuming their dream walk, spreading out casually as they abandoned what was left of the body behind.

I felt my limbs go numb, comprehension of what this meant seeping into my brain. *There went our shot*, I thought panicked. *Thirteen days and that fool had to try to talk to them*. I ran my hands over my face, the idea of spending thirteen more days here forcing my fingernails into my cheeks. The pain felt nice, bringing me to my senses long enough to reach into the bag and pull out my Glock.

I played with the trigger for a moment. *You still don't know why Kelesa and Kara died*, I thought. *Put it away. A few more days, just a few more days.*

But you'll end up like that, a different thought challenged, my eyes laser-sighting toward the fresh corpse. I felt my hand tighten on the gun as I turned away only to see hordes of vipers. *Or like them.*

It took my brain far too long to realize that one of the vipers looked different. She was standing still, trembling from head to toe, tears running down her cheeks, mortified by the corpse on the ground. I could see the effort it took to fight the sounds of her jarring breaths, and she wasn't going to last long.

Eyes wide with disbelief I slowly moved into a crouching position. Had she come through with the man or after? Had she just seen the dead body or had she witnessed the vipers in action?

Don't move, I thought desperately. *Don't move. Come on Victor, you have to see her.* As the seconds crawled by I started to worry that Victor had come to the same conclusion I had and seen our only chance taken away.

After an eternity of razor silence I knew Victor had finally snapped. He'd given into whatever was haunting him, and now I was alone. It was a choice between hiding and dying, but in this case hiding was dying, only slower. My choice made, I tried to figure out a signal that wouldn't startle her, but before I could even begin, her single sniffle seemed to set off every viper in the city.

I went ridged with horror, her face turning whiter than the moon, the wails piercing both body and soul, but then, miraculously, the machine-gun fire blared on the other end of the field, consuming the night with nightmares of war.

Chapter 7

The vipers were in frenzy, lashing out zealously in the direction of the machine gun, but a few still remembered the fresh prize only a few feet away. Almost too fast to see, a short haired brunette was on the newcomer, twisting at her head in a motion only meant to kill. Another was sinking its fingernails into her arm while screaming his previous victim's blood on her face.

I hesitated only for a second, my minds fear of being heard fighting against my will, but I shot at the brunette with my Glock. The bullet hit the side of her head, likely because I was afraid of hitting the victim, but it was enough to drop her to the ground. The shot felt like thunder despite the rapid bark of the machine gun, but the second viper didn't care as it pushed the woman to the ground, snapping at her with his teeth.

Grabbing the crossbow, I stepped out from the bushes, exposing myself to the world and fired the steel tipped bolt into the back of the viper's neck. The pain barely seemed relevant to the viper as he continued his assault. I flung myself onto the viper and by the time I wrestled him away from the woman he was dead from asphyxiation.

The woman's fingernails racked across my forearm as I reached down to make sure she was okay, but my reaction to the stinging pain gave her enough pause to see that I wasn't trying to kill her. I put a finger to my lips, hoping she hadn't forgotten silence, and then pulled her to her feet.

Victor, sweet, sweet, son of the devil, Victor, had made his distraction in the opposite direction of the pawn shop so that we could b-line it to safety, but we hadn't counted on how many vipers it would attract. As I dragged the woman behind me, vipers from every corner of Central Park were crawling and running toward the sound, but sound didn't compare to flesh covered and vulnerable regulars like us.

I emptied my magazine in the first minute as we ran across the lawn toward the street, and slid in the second while wishing the pawn shop dealt in more black market gear like grenades and rocket launchers. A literal wall of vipers swarmed toward Victor's position, and the only good at the moment was that the woman didn't fight against me dragging her.

"Let's hope this works," I said flipping Victor's Zippo-lighter open. The pawn shop was packed with all sorts of goodies, and thanks to the NRA we had pounds of gunpowder. On my way into the park the past five days I'd trailed bottles of the stuff behind me, hiding cans of gasoline below trees and bushes. I stunk to high heaven, and it had made the sneaking around harder, but if we got lucky enough to find a survivor… well right now we I needed a safe way out.

I threw the lighter, and as soon as it hit the spot I'd marked, haphazard streams and blotches of fire appeared, setting off a mine field of tiny flames across the lawn. The flames grew weak quickly, but the fire startled the vipers, sending them into screams of terror, and a few moments later the gas cans exploded, the push of the blast waves aiding us in our escape.

Mercifully the viper's fear of fire was extreme, and what took over an hour crawling in silence, only took two minutes sprinting.

Afraid of moving away from the safety of the fire, I forced myself to tuck the Glock into the back of my pants, reload the crossbow, and duck into the shadows of the alley streets.

"Where are we going?" the woman whispered breathlessly. I was surprised at how easily I could hear her, but then I realized Victor's gun fire had stopped.

"Somewhere safe," I whispered back. "Just stay low and watch your step."

I dragged her somewhat ruthlessly down a back alley that I'd used multiple times, and it only figured that one of the vipers would have wandered to that exact spot at the exact time. The crossbow took him in eye, but not before the inhuman screech boomed from his throat.

"Don't look back, just run," I whispered, panic lacing every word as I pulled her into a sprint. "If you see fire, get to it, it's our only chance."

My body was already exhausted when the vipers began emerging from their hiding spots like some kind of military ambush. Our head start didn't last long, and it was only seconds before one ripped through the back of my jacket in an attempt to tackle me to the ground.

Then, with the next attack, I did hit the ground. I grabbed the Glock on the way down, but my head struck the street with a loud thud, and without realizing it I pointed the gun at the woman behind me. My mind froze for just a moment; an accident better left forgotten flashing in my vision as the vipers began dragging her back by her legs. Shaken, I watched as she desperately dug her nails into the ground to avoid being taken, her scream only serving to enrage the vipers. I tried to wash away my blurry vision, but my finger reacted before my brain did. I felt the recoil from the pistol shots, terror about what I'd just done giving me just enough clarity to see that I'd managed to turn the gun before the trigger had done its magic. I stumbled forward, pulling her free as the two vipers fell from their bullet wounds.

I nearly toppled over as I dragged her back to her feet, immediately made aware that she'd been hurt and couldn't walk. I could see the bonfire just around the corner, but we weren't going to make it in time on her legs so I emptied the rest of the clip into the crowd of vipers and pulled her into a fireman's hold, ordering my shaking legs to move toward the sanctuary of the light.

I remembered making it through the pawn shops door before my head recalled that it had smashed against asphalt. I remembered the faces of the viper's as the light from the liberating fire seemed to burn them, but worst of all, before blacking out, I remembered that the woman I'd just saved had naturally colored red hair, exactly Victor Herse's type.

Chapter 8

The euphoric giggle of a young girl brought me back from whatever void I had fallen into. I could feel my lips pull up into a smile as I pictured Kara running around the house, terrorizing her mother. The smell of seared chicken teased my senses, and my stomach growled as I opened my eyes.

"Kelesa?" I whispered as she smiled down on me.

"Who?" The woman said, my illusion shattering into a million pieces as the pawn shop behind her came into focus.

My mind clawed its way out of the fog surprisingly fast and I sat up, my eyes darting around for any sign of Victor. "Has anyone else shown up," I asked quickly, startling the woman as I pushed her aside.

"No," she stammered, "I haven't seen anyone since the others turned away."

I felt a little dizzy moving toward the counter, but I found the shotgun left behind the counter for emergencies and checked that it was loaded. My attention then immediately turned toward the fire, but it looked like it had just been fueled with a pile of books we kept stacked in the back. Then I noticed the woman. Her face was splotched black allowing tears streaks to use it as a canvas. She was in her late twenties, thin, and strikingly beautiful. Her bottom lip was bigger than the top, giving her a soft sensual look even while she was grimacing with pain. She wore a simple halter top and jeans, the left leg of which had been torn completely off, exposing pale creamy flesh above a blood soaked rag.

"I couldn't find any thread to sew it shut," she said, noticing my concern. The wound had to have stretched the length of her calf for it to bleed that much.

I slid open a drawer and tossed her a spool of black thread that we'd used to patch our clothes. "You have a needle?"

She held up a thin silver piece of metal and nodded with a wince. "Already sterilized."

"What's your name?" I asked, moving around the counter and toward the door.

She started un-wrapping the bandage, confirming that the viper's had torn a canyon sized gash down the middle of her calf muscle. "Catherine. You're that detective that was on the news a few years ago. Jared, something—"

"The joys of television," I mumbled as I scanned the street from inside the door. There were a few vipers shuffling around, but no sign that any normal person was close by.

She hissed through the pain as she pushed the needle through her skin. "Thanks for saving me."

"Sorry I couldn't help the other guy," I mumbled sympathetically, remembering the mangle wreck the vipers had discarded.

A fresh tear ran down her blackened cheek, dropping onto her shaking hands. "Blake," she said heavily. "He was a surgeon like me. We'd started dating about a month ago." She looked up suddenly, and the hatred in her eyes was palpable. "Why did they kill him?"

"They kill everyone," I said walking away from the door. As I moved toward the fire I noticed her hands still trembling; she was either the world's worst surgeon or I needed to change the subject. "How long was I out?"

"About an hour," Catherine hissed. "You have a pretty bad concussion—you should stay off your feet. Where are we by the way?" She growled the last question as she tied off the thread and finished pulling the wound closed.

"As far as I know we are inside Saints Tower. I assume the last thing you did was walk through the door?"

"I think so," she said slowly, "I remember the tower and the door, but I don't remember going in. We were listening to the Wise Ones..."

"What?" I asked, noticing the subtle signs that she'd remember something, but didn't want to share.

"There was someone there, a rich man by the look of it; he whispered the name of my son as he walked by. That's why I followed him. Blake tried to stop me, and when he couldn't he went in first... I...it's my fault."

"Why would hearing your son's name make you—"

A cool breezed blasted into the room, coaxing the bonfire into a wild dance of survival. My eyes darted toward the door and I raised the shotgun.

"You'll never believe what—"Victor eyes crooked as he noticed the weapon pointed at his head. His eyes traveled from the gun to Catherine, and in that one-second glace I knew he understood. He hid his desire well, I was probably the only one in the world that could have seen it, but he also looked tired. His features were ghostly as if he was slowly turning to dust. Even his malevolent grin looked weak.

"It's been awhile since we've had visitors," Victor said kindly. "I've told you a hundred times, Jared—the vipers won't come near this here fire—no reason to go all lethal. I'd like to introduce myself to this lovely young lady if I may."

"I don't think that's a good idea," I said warningly.

"Oh the sweetness I'm imagining right now would haunt your dreams, Jared, but we have bigger fish to fry." He winked at Catherine, dismissing my tightening grip. "I don't know about you, but I actually think I stepped over the edge today."

"What's going on here?" Catherine interrupted.

Victor looked at Catherine and grinned. "Well sweetums, Jared and I here... well we threw a hailmary. Guess what we caught?"

Alarm bells must have rang in Catherine's mind because she immediately tensed, her pain transforming into a phantom as she looked from me to Victor.

"That's right," Victor said moving to sit in his chair. "We got ourselves a genuine innocent. Now we can get out of this nightmare."

"What's he talking about, Jared?" She asked pleadingly.

I hated myself for lowering the shotgun, but I didn't look away from Victor as I answered. "This tower is treating us like prisoners—you're the key to getting out of this place."

"Why me?" she asked.

"Because you haven't killed a viper yet," Victor said joyfully, standing and spreading his arms wide as if to preach to a congregation. "In this land of crazy and darkness, you are the only saint amongst the damned. Now lead us—I beg of you darling—to that heavenly door."

Chapter 9

Catherine listened to Victor as he explained his plan, but it was only a distraction for her. I'd been where she was, the body and mind still confused about how such a big piece of your life was gone. It was a lot to put on her after Blake's death, but I knew that anything was better than acknowledging that emptiness, so I went along with it.

"You expect me to hear voices and then to follow them?" Catherine asked incredulously as she heated up a can of Spagetti'Os.

"I know," I said defensively. "It's not much to go on, but it's all we have. Every time we try to ask the woman in black for answers she flees from us."

"Maybe she'll talk to me?" Catherine suggested, testing her first bite for heat.

I shrugged. "We can try, but that means going back outside with the vipers. And trust me, Catherine, when you start to worry that your own heartbeat is going to set off the zombie apocalypse, leaving the shop becomes a last resort."

"Usually, hearing voices is a bad sign," she said skeptically, but I could tell that she was nervous. She kept avoiding eye contact and was giving her can of food too much attention. "How do I even know you're telling the truth? Maybe I'm just dreaming."

"That sounded confident," Victor laughed. "Girl, your boyfriend has already been eaten. I suggest you start praying you hear the voices sooner rather than later."

'I hate agreeing with him," I sighed, "but he's right. You wouldn't think it, but Victor is only in his early thirties." Catherine skepticism faltered when she saw Victor's gray mane of hair and wrinkly skin. "We're all on a clock," I added. "Tick tock. You need to trust us."

Catherine dropped the can of Spagetti'Os, the aluminum can clanging on the ground a few times before coming to a stop. I was afraid I'd scared her, but her attention was on her shaking hands.

"Are you sure you're a surgeon?" I asked.

"Of course I am," she said bitterly. "I'm just… afraid, okay." She gave a little laugh. "My grandmother suffered from dementia when I was a little girl. I could remember her talking to herself, whispering secrets about old neighbors…"

Victor nearly fell out of his seat as he sat up. "What are you saying girl? Spit it out."

Catherine gulped and stared into the fire, a sudden icy fear seeping into behavior. "I don't want to hear things that aren't there. I won't."

Victor looked at Catherine murderously, but I held up a warning hand and turned back to Catherine. "You already hear the voices—don't you?" I whispered hopefully.

She didn't answer, but I could tell I had guessed right based on the set of her jaw.

"What are they saying?" I asked eagerly, looking toward Victor, who was busily trying to find something to write on.

"I knew the plan would work," he mumbled. "See Sid, I told you. Find an innocent and—"

My excitement waned as Victor's rambling caused Catherine to pull her knees up to her chest and shelter herself in her arms. "Stop it!" she shouted, shaking her head. "Stop being happy that I'm going crazy. I've seen were it leads."

Victor stopped shuffling through the desk and looked toward Catherine. "Crazy is relative," he smiled. "But in this case, crazy is our salvation."

"Shut up, Herse," I growled, putting a hand on Catherine's shoulder. "You're not crazy. It's the tower, it's not you. There something off about this place, you can't let it get to you."

I listened to her sobs for a while as I mulled over my present company. *The tower makes everyone crazy, I thought, everyone. Catherine hasn't even been here a day and Victor's been fighting off madness for weeks. How much has it affected me? I want Catherine to listen to voices in her head, for heaven sakes, to follow them to some unknown guardian and door. I've followed the plans of a serial killer, I've let him spend time with his ideal victim, and you're killing vipers without batting an eye. Oh your crazy alright, probably more crazy then all of them.*

"I'm not crazy!" I shouted suddenly, my tongue lashing out of control. I grimaced at the sight I must have presented, and put my head in my hands, shaking it. I didn't even look up at Catherine as I pleaded, "We need to get out of here, Catherine. This tower does something to you. I came here to find out why the tower killed my family, but I can barely focus on that now. I still want... need to understand, but we have to get out of here first. You're my only chance at that."

"But the towers good," Catherine said carefully. "It saved Blake's life. It helped me find my family again...This can't be the tower."

"Oh, boy," Victor said. "She's a believer."

"That doesn't matter now," I cut off. "All that matters is whether she helps us or not." I took a deep breath. "Do the voices say anything about a door?"

Catherine nodded slowly, sad eyes staring into mine. "They are telling me not to tell you. They say you seek to destroy the tower."

I wasn't sure where or when Catherine had found the small pistol, but it only took a moment for her to pull it out and train it on my head. She still looked frightened and confused, but I couldn't help but notice that her hands had stopped shaking. "I'm sorry, Jared."

Chapter 10

"Catherine," I whispered gently, putting my hands up. "What are you doing?"

"They are telling me to kill you," she said in a harsh whisper. "They say I can see Blake again—that you are forsaken."

"I wouldn't do that if I were you miss," Victor said as he sighted his own pistol on Catherine.

"Herse, put the gun down. She not going to shoot me," I said carefully. It was as if an entirely different person had taken over Catherine's body, but I was banking on that hollow feeling I could still see in her eyes. "Blake's dead Catherine, you saw it yourself—killed by the things that live in this tower. We saved you remember. You said it yourself; you didn't want to listen to the voices. Why would you listen to them if they are telling you to kill someone? Have you ever even considered killing someone before?"

"You can't find the door without me," she said possessed. "It'll only open for me—it will only welcome me if I kill you."

"You sure about her, Jared," Victor said challengingly. "She's losing it pretty darn fast." I wasn't sure anymore, the grin that was growing on her face was bordering on insane or super villain.

"Catherine, listen to me," I said firmly. "You mentioned something about hearing your son's name before coming into the tower. You never told me why that made you come into the tower. Is he also in here?"

Catherine pupils sank into tiny beads of black and the gun began to tremble in her hand. "Aaron," she whispered. "That man said Aaron was here. He promised me, where is he?"

There was a moment of hesitation as she seemed to listen to something unseen, but it was all I needed. I bolted toward her, twisting the gun from her hand before she could react. She screamed murderously as she was knocked to the floor by Victor.

"She's flipping, Jared!" Victor screamed, as he pinned Catherine's thrashing arms behind her.

"The door! The door! The door!" she wailed as she fought against Victor's grip. "Aaron is behind the door."

"We gotta put her down," Victor grunted as she head-butted his jaw. "She's going viper."

I bent down on my knees, being sure to keep the weapon out of her reach, and grabbed her chin in my other hand. "Catherine!" I shouted, slapping her in the face. "You said your son is in here, well, let's go find him!"

Her eyes, wild and unforced before, zeroed in on mine and stuck. "We'll go right now," I said slowly. "If he's still alive in this place he has to be through the door. What do ya say?"

"They'll try to stop you," Catherine said hoarsely. "The guardian is in the way."

"But it won't stop you, will it?" I said tossing Victor a hopeful look.

"No," she said heavily, her eyes drooping. 'It will let me pass. I can hear it calling me, it wants me." Her eyes fell shut, and her breathing grew heavy.

"Catherine," I said shaking her gently. "Where is it?"

"Dark tunnel, bright lights, 81st street," she mumbled.

Suddenly, Catherine's eyes snapped open, and it was as if someone else was there. "I'm not supposed to tell you," she laughed fanatically, her face twisting in an unnatural smile. "It's a secret, it's a secret—"

I felt guilty at the sound of the sickening thud that the butt of my gun produced against her skull, but unconsciousness immediately soothed the madness that was taking over.

"It's about time," Victor panted, dropping her to the floor. "Bodies not what it used to be—should have just let me shoot her."

"We got an address," I said through dry lips. "And I'll be the judge of who we kill or don't kill."

Victor chuckled as he freed himself of Catherine's weight. "That because you're a cop?"

"No, it's because it's not the first thing on my mind. At least part of her tried to help us."

`"Fair enough, fair enough," he said yawning, "but you're carrying the joker."

Chapter 11

We weren't sure what version of Catherine we'd meet when she woke up, so we didn't wait. I thought Victor would be opposed to taking Catherine with us, but to my surprise he never argued, immediately making me suspicious. I hoped getting her away from this place would help, but Victor kept eyeing the girl like she was some kind of trophy as we gathered our stuff together. Victor was rather protective of his backpack, hiding its contents as I handed him his lighter back. He tested to see if it still worked, but only shrugged when it failed to produce a flame, tossing it in with the other junk in his bag. I was confused about the broken alarm clock sitting on the top, but he shut the bag as soon as he noticed I was looking.

"What's with all the wires and junk?" I asked as I grabbed for the crossbow.

Victor slapped my hand away. "None of your business—and this one's mine. Not my fault you dropped yours in the park."

"Extreme possessiveness come packaged with psychopathic?" I said annoyed. "Relax Herse, it's not a like I'm an infamous thief."

Victor took a deep breath. "I know, it just...having that girl around is making me uncomfortable. She's a random factor. I don't like random. You ready?"

I nodded, trying to ignore the fact that she probably made him uncomfortable in different ways as well, and zipped up my duffle bag.

I hoped it was just psychological, but the air seemed glittered with frost when we stepped outside the shop. The cold was alive, seeping into my flesh like needles, and making Catherine's body feel dead against my shoulder. Victor grunted worriedly through his beard as caught and grinded a piece of frost between his fingers.

We're gonna freeze, I thought as I started walking down the street barefoot.

The hollow air made every sound travel for miles, and unfortunately 81st street was near Central Park. It was slow going while carrying another human being, but we were able to use most of the less viper infested paths until the park was in view.

The vipers were unaffected by the cold weather, which felt unfair considering they had all the sweaters and coats. As usual they paid no attention to anything, but my concern that Catherine could wake up at anytime made wish I'd hit her harder. Her heavy breathing already sounded as if a steam engine was moving down the street.

Victor motioned for me to follow him south, and it didn't take long for us to reach the Museum of Natural History. Its shadowed pillars could have hidden any number of vipers from view so we stopped a short distance away. 81st wasn't enormous, but the idea of scouting the entire street for a door wasn't encouraging. Victor eyes were intent on the Museum, telling me that he was hoping he didn't have to make the dangerous trip either. Warming up before going any further was more than just simple comfort, it was survival.

I found my mind instinctively looking for a car despite the fact I hadn't seen any in weeks. This place was usually swarming with car, bike, and people traffic, but I could only see two vipers slugging their way down the street. Kelesa always hated coming to visit me at work; rush hour traffic was the biggest thing she hated about the city. Benjamin's office was two blocks from here and when she'd get off the…

Dark tunnel, bright lights, 81st street; that's it! I thought. My numb feet suddenly remembered the cold as I turned to look further up the street, the sensation of being watched settling somewhere near the bottom of my gut. I took a moment, resting Catherine against the nearest wall, debating whether my idea was even a possibility. Then I tapped Victor on the shoulder, and pointed. His first reaction was a gradual tense of muscles, but then a dreadful shiver crawled over him as he watched three vipers descend the steps into the 81st subway station.

He shook his head incredulously, hoping to dispel the idea, but it wasn't enough. His grimace soon afterward told me he knew it was the only answer as well.

It was hard to believe that just a few weeks ago this spot had been warm under the spring rain, but right now the aching cold only discouraged me to lift Catherine and moving forward. Victor followed behind me. I didn't have to see his expression to know it was the same as mine, determined. We were going to find that door, even if it killed us.

The mouth of the stairwell devoured the moonlight after only a few steps down, and I couldn't help but jerk to a stop. No fire, no electricity, and no light; only darkness, vipers, and who knew what else lurked beneath the ground. I could hear strange unnatural sobs travel up at me, prickling at my skin like fleas. My chest felt hollow and my mind begged me to go back to the pawn shops warmth.

It's just a subway, I told myself, taking a deep breath.

Victor struck a match, sending a small ripping sound throughout the city. I clinched my jaw, readying to run, but Victor just calmly tried to ignite a makeshift torch made from torn book pages, decayed mattress foam, and old butane.

As the windblown flame licked the paper, I braced for the world to explode into wailing, but they never came. Instead, the torch began to burn, casting just enough light that we might be able see in front of us. Victor seemed encouraged by the fire, sliding the shotgun off his shoulder while taking the first few steps into darkness. I wasn't so sure. That sound should have had us in panic mode, fleeing for our lives—something was off.

Moving after him, I grabbed the Glock from my waist as the twisted sobs and whispers grew louder with each step. I wasn't sure what we would see, but the gargling, guttural sounds climbing the stairwell started coming from Catherine as well.

Then the torch winked out, and like some nocturnal creature, Catherine shift awake on my shoulder, her chest heaved as if she was crying, the sound coming from her throat that of a strangled cat. I twisted my shoulder down to drop her to the ground, but suddenly the dark reached out and sunk its claws into my ankle.

Chapter 12

In an invisible world I sensed the blackness spin, feeling each step on the way down, some in my ribs, others against my spine. The pain was sharp and quick, but so was the fall. I landed on my stomach, arms braced beneath me to soften the fall. A billowing cloud of dust had exploded from the air knocked from my lungs, tickling my nose.

It took all of my concentration to get in a single breath as I rolled onto my back in pain, but when I did I saw Victor's torch laying on the ground next me. Its light was faint beneath the dust, but it was enough to show me Victor's alert face. He was lying on the ground, obviously in as much pain as I was, but his gaze was looking through me.

I coughed several times, but froze as dozens of human shadows scurried across the ground like rats around the torch. My hand shot to my belt, searching for the Glock, but I'd dropped the gun during the fall. I cringed as I moved my hand, feeling that I'd either broken or jammed some fingers.

I recoiled as I felt someone grab my arm, my muffled scream bringing wails from the shadows.

"The door," Catherine's voice whispered. "I can see it, come on Detective."

I let what I hoped was Catherine, pull me to my feet, and turned to grab Victor's torch. When I turned back to Catherine what I saw made me lash out with the torch like some wild crazed mental patient. The three faces looming behind her looked like they'd been crafted from horror, twisted in some brutal forge of ugly.

The fire sent the creatures reeling back into the shadows, but Catherine's bloodcurdling scream at my attack drove all the shadows in the room into frenzy. The gagging, throat vomiting sounds doubled in volume, and I watched as Catherine started walking toward them, convulsing oddly as she moved.

"Jared," Victor's voice said in a panicked whisper. "She was right. The door... I can see the torch reflecting off of it. Start moving, I'll follow you."

I grabbed Catherine by the arm with my good hand, bruising her under my grip as I hauled her toward the reflections. Shadows lashed out at my legs, nearly knocking me to the ground, but I fought them off with the torch as best I could until I crashed into a pillar. I fumbled the torch, barely catching it as two creatures leapt from the darkness, trapping me against the concrete.

Victor's shotgun took the first in the head, blowing him back into the darkness, but the second turned on him, wrestling the shotgun away before I used the torch like a baseball bat to knock it away. Catherine still sounded like she was choking, but she managed to grab my shoulder as we moved forward, jumping the toll booth to get to the subway.

The doors looked exactly like they did on the outside, silver and white, like the gates of heaven, two mirrors on each ornate monstrosity, only every feature was twisted in the darkness. And as if to mock me, or torture me, at its head it read, *Saints Tower Second Floor*.

How many floors are there?! My mind screamed.

The face of the woman in black suddenly appeared in the torchlight, sending me stumbling back into Victor. She laughed wickedly sweet as she placed herself in front of the door like some gargoyle of righteousness.

"Oh crap," I said stupidly as I panting for breath. In silence I watched as hands from the shadows began reaching out to her wantonly, like a starved beggar would for food. The creatures longed for her, and yet, despite the gruesome company the woman looked gentle, just as before.

"You should not have made it this far," the woman said astonished.

"Why not?" I said shakily as Catherine continued gagging next to me.

The woman fell to her knees and spread out her arms, letting the creatures run their hands across her skin. "You are trespassers."

"That's funny," Victor said from behind, "I didn't see a sign anywhere."

"The woman Catherine may pass," the woman in black said calmly, her head bowing slightly. "She has not harmed the others, but you two are not prepared. You are much like these ones that hide in the dark, any chance at moving on barred from them. Sadly, in time this will be your fate. The death of your wife and child plagues your heart, Jared Reign—there will be no peace ahead. And poor Victor, such potential wasted, a mind harassed by the regulations of caution. You long for that which was never yours, losing yourself with each passing moment of a broken heart. Such a weakness will haunt you forever."

"What do you want?" I asked harshly. "Who are you really?"

"I am the guardian of this portal, a last chance and a guide for the lost," she whispered. "But I cannot guide you. If you step through this door you will ruin greatness. One cannot simply force his way to the top. Your actions touch too many others. It is foolish to allow such choices to run rampant."

There was a drawn out silence as the guardian closed her eyes and bowed in meditation. As both a parent and a police officer I'd learned a lot about silences. Whether it was Kara playing with an electrical outlet or booking a thug for selling drugs, it always meant trouble. I didn't know what was coming this time, but there was only one answer to stop your kid from shocking themselves or from a thugs buddy shooting at you from the next street over—act first.

I pulled Catherine in front of me like a shield and pushed her toward the woman, walking quickly. Catherine tried to fight back, but I held on firmly and charged forward. When the guardian lifted her head, I could sense an enormous danger coming, but I also saw surprise in her eyes at the sight of Catherine. The surprise only lasted a few seconds, but it gave me enough time to see the knives she had drawn in each hand. The creatures on either side began fighting between their love of the siren and their hatred of the torch moving closer to them.

I fought against my instinct to protect Catherine and moved her in the way of the first attack from the guardian. I wasn't sure whether to shout forgiveness, mercy, or thanks to every god or deity I'd ever heard of, but as I'd suspected the guardian reared her attack away just before striking Catherine. I followed up with a swing of the torch, twisting me and Catherine behind the guardian, but the woman moved like a wraith, floating into a maneuver that seemed impossible. Her knife slashed between Catherine's arm and torso, piercing the side of my hip, forcing me to fall to one knee. I kept Catherine wrapped close to me as the woman went for another attack, but it wasn't going to be enough.

Victor slammed into the woman, his shoulder picking the woman up into the air as he collided into her chest. Unfortunately the move didn't seem to pain the woman, only allowing us a few seconds of time as she scrambled to her feet.

I lost my grip on Catherine as I limped toward the door, but the woman in black was already racing toward me. Victor was still standing, trying to push open the door, but he seemed to be struggling. I felt the knife pierce my shoulder before I could turn back, but I continued moving forward, touching the base of the door with my palm.

I mustered what strength I could, and pushed with Victor. It took a few seconds for the door to begin inching open, but when the white light appeared I looked up into the mirror. What I saw shocked me. The woman I'd just used as a human shield was now standing between me and the guardian, preventing her from finishing me off.

"Move you foolish girl," the guardian demanded. "You have no idea what you're doing."

"Catherine, it's open," I moaned. "Go."

Catherine took two careful steps back before running, but the corrupted vipers leapt onto her, pinning her down as the woman in black marched toward me. I managed to hurl my duffle bag at the guardian, catching her by surprise as the objects inside scattered across the room. I hoped I'd given Victor enough time to hit her again, but he was already stepping through the door. I felt my energy being sapped as my shoulder and gut bled on the floor. *He's going to leave us here*, I thought panicked.

"You Bas—"I screamed, cut off by the sensation of the knife stabbing through my shin bone and calf muscle, nailing me to the floor. I screamed, and out of desperation, my hands scrambled across the floor grabbing for a weapon, anything. My fingers fumbled against something and I looked down to see a small can of gasoline that had fallen free from my duffle bag. Quickly I unscrew the cap throwing the contents over the woman. The action confused her long enough for me to get my fingers around the torch, and as she moved in for the kill I stabbed it against her black skirt, flames spreading across her body almost immediately.

The woman in black looked down at me annoyed, and my veins felt like shaved ice despite the sweltering flames consuming her being only inches away. "That is very impolite," she said.

"Screw manners," I said, kicking out with my free leg. The blow hit her in the stomach, sending her stumbling back far enough that the vipers holding Catherine down fled from the flames.

The woman's recovery was fast, but then two crossbow bolts hit her in the chest. I turned at the clamber of footsteps behind me, and saw Victor's eyes darting between me and the guardian as he scrambled to load another bolt. Catherine crawled passed the stunned woman in black, and for a moment she looked just like the vipers. "I don't care," she said shaking her head. "Stop shouting at me! You're lying, you're lying."

"Catherine!" I shouted.

The woman in black grabbed Catherine by the hair, twisting her around and pulling her close so that they were face to face. "Listen to the voices, girl. They are your only chance now." Oddly, she threw Catherine toward me falling to her knees a moment later, grasping at the crossbow bolts. "You'll regret killing me. Without me they are all lost, and daddy... he'll be very angry."

It took him longer than it should have, but eventually Victor pulled the knife out of my leg and hooked his hands under my armpits, dragging me backward. "I don't understand," the woman in black said coughing. "I just wanted to help. Then...you showed up... Why? What do you want Jared Reign?"

"I want to know why my family was killed!" I shouted back viciously.

Catherine crawled after me, only stopping to look back when the woman in black's body hit the floor.   I could practically taste the regret in Catherine's eyes as she moved passed me. She might have thought she was doing the right thing, but she was definitely struggling against something.

"Deeper down the rabbit hole," Victor said, stepping into the door's light after Catherine. "With any luck we'll meet this *daddy*."

Chapter 13

The only thing I was aware of was standing. I could feel my feet touching the ground, but I couldn't see beyond the blazing sun hanging high in the sky. Its heat felt like hot tar against my skin, coaxing out waves of sweat like some cruel sauna. My eyes squinted as the world rippled with the heat rays, distorting blocky images and creating ten years worth of crow's feet. What I didn't notice was any pain. I knew I'd been stabbed, but as my hands stumbled across my body searching for blood or torn flesh, they couldn't find any.

My mind suddenly clicked on, and from past experience I dropped my hands immediately, shut my mouth, tried to breathe as little as possible, and held perfectly still. My vision was adjusting; bringing blurred movements to life which meant a viper could be standing only a few feet away.

It only took a few moments for the rest of my senses to tell me what my eyes were missing. My skin started to tingle, my ears howled with wind, and I felt my nose twitch with irritation as I drew in breathes of dirt or sand. I felt my lungs rebel at the idea, and as hard as I tried I couldn't stop the coughing.

"Don't worry," whispered a soft feminine voice. "The storm will pass soon."

"Not soon enough," I heard Victor shout. "It tastes like cockroaches."

As if on cue the whistling air began to fade away, and within a matter of minutes the air became completely clear. What I saw was extraordinary. I was once again standing in the middle of central park, but New York looked like it had adopted Egyptian culture. Palm trees stood around the northern lake, people dressed in robes of white and brown, and the buildings were beautified by lush vines and pink and purple lotus flowers.

"Welcome friends. It is good that you have made it this far. I have little taste for the first floor. It is a bleak existence."

"Whoa," Victor breathed, summing up my thoughts on the woman standing in front of us. She had soft fair skin, flowing brunette hair, glistening red lips, and no eyes. It wasn't as if here eye sockets were empty, there simply wasn't any evidence that eyes belonged on her face, like an artist hadn't finished painting her. Eyes usually told the most about people, especially when interrogating them or first meeting them, but her expression was off; her smile was too forced, her eyebrows too accented, almost as if they were making up for not having the preverbal windows to the soul. However, I felt a certain lure toward her and could sense a familiar sensual grace as she moved toward us.

"Yes, Jared," she said, holding her hand out toward me like a queen. "I am indeed like my sister below—your guide and protector." Speckles of red decorated her arm, glittering like rubies under the sun, but despite the beauty of it I took a step back.

As if accustomed to being worshipped by newcomers, her shock lit up like warning bells and I quickly changed my mind, stepped forward, bowed before the woman, and kissed her hand. It tasted like roses, and surprisingly it took an effort of will to pull my lips away. I was quickly growing worried. She'd known my name, known that I was comparing her to the woman in black, but for some reason she'd expected certain affections from us. Maybe she was unaware of her sister's failure to stop us, or maybe she didn't care.

The woman's soft smile was probably meant to relax me, give me hope that she'd bought my act, but there was always the chance that she was just a better actor.

"My name is Loral, child," she said graciously. "It is my pleasure to welcome you to my rapture. Come, get cleaned up, and relax with me for a time—then I will teach you the way."

Turning, Loral motioned for us to follow, but a high pitch ringing in the distance caught my attention and I turned, searching for its origin. It was the first time I'd seen Victor and Catherine since entering the door, and I couldn't help but flinch back. Covered in filth and dressed casually in a ripped and torn sports jacket, Victor's wild bronze beard failed to hide that he looked forty years younger. Catherine's long, fiery red curls dropping across the exposed charred flesh of her now shoulder-less black top. They looked broken, ready to kill over at the slightest push, but their missing eyes, those were what really worried me.

"Victor!" I cried out, my hands shooting up to my eyes as the ringing in the distance grew louder. I cringed as I poked my eyes, but the relief I felt was worth it.

Victor seemed as shocked as I did, his hands mimicking mine, but before he could respond, the ringing became recognizable, and in the next moment a woman darted from the trees, terror attacking her face, screaming as if some wild beast was hunting her.

She ran straight towards us, stumbling across the lawn because her legs wouldn't move as fast as she wanted. It was probably a fool's move, but I started toward the woman. I only made it two steps before something hit her in the neck, immediately sending her crashing to the ground like a narcoleptic ragdoll.

When I reached the woman she was face down, breathing deeply, and as I turned her over I noticed two things. First a six inch tribal dart was sticking out from the side of her neck, and second she had blue eyes. I watched as they looked at me desperately before rolling into the back of her skull, but what concerned me the most were the red tears falling down her cheeks.

"She will be alright," Loral said, her soothing voice relaxing me as she approached from behind with Victor and Catherine. "This is the work of that horrible woman. Come now, my servant Beltin will see to her safety."

"Her eyes are bleeding," Catherine said surprised.

"Beltin!" Loral called loudly. "See that no one else is lured away today, and please take Naomi to safety."

A few yards away, a man in a World War II uniform dropped from one of the palm trees. He was young, only a corporal according to his tags, and like everyone else beside Naomi, eyeless.

"Yes, Ma'am," he said, giving Loral a proper salute and pocketing what looked like a thin tube. "I will do my best." Bending down to Naomi, he smiled at the grip I had on the woman and asked, "May I?"

"You shot her with a blow dart gun?" I asked incredulously.

He nodded. "Better than a bullet."

It took me a few moments of staring at his eyeless face to release the woman, but he merely waited patiently until he was allowed to scoop her into his arms. Turning on his boots, he gave Loral one last nod and ran off in the opposite direction.

"Well ain't that some—"Victor started, but was stopped when Loral put a hand on his shoulder. I could tell he fought the urge to pull away, and for the first time I was happy Victor had a sharp mind.

"I am sorry you had to see this," Loral said, her lips practically pouting. "Occasionally we have those that stray, but I assure you this is rare, pay it little attention. It is your path that is important."

"My path?" Victor asked.

"You wish to climb the tower, do you not?"

"I'm starting to question that choice," Victor said doubtfully.

"You can always choose to stay with me if not," Loral smiled. "But you should know that the door will only reveal itself to those who serve. Like Beltin, you must show your worthiness."

I wasn't sure what Victor's glance toward me meant. Without eyes it could have been anything, but

I was hoping for fear. Some serious voodoo was going on, and my gut told me that this desert utopia might be worse than the city locked in darkness. *Saints Tower Second Floor*, I thought as we began following Loral, *what does that even mean.*

Chapter 14

We didn't walk far before another sandstorm hit, but Loral was able to guide us into what looked like a hotel before its full intensity blinded us. Decorated like Cleopatra's bedroom, the large lobby was covered in lush pillows and silky cloth; not only on the floor, but draped across the walls and ceiling. Three women, wearing what I would have sworn were Princess Leia costumes, greeted us and started blowing the sand off us with giant fans.

"This is nice," I heard Catherine whisper.

"Frightening," Victor said, "Not nice."

I tried to scan the room for any grasp of reality, but my mind kept turning back to Catherine. I wasn't sure what to think about her. Victor, I thought I understood as much as was possible, but I wasn't even sure I'd met Catherine. Her behavior was flip flopping, and without her eyes I wasn't even sure she was confused by anything that was going on. She'd practically saved my life by interfering with the woman in black, but there was no way to know if she was still hearing voices, or worse, doing their bidding. The three of us needed some alone time, but if my undercover buddies had taught me anything, I had to follow the script and hope I got lucky later.

"I will arrange a room for each of you," Loral said excitedly. "In the mean time, please sit and relax." She showed us to a section of cushions occupied by two other eyeless people who were having a quiet conversation. They seemed excited about what they'd done last night, sharing embarrassed whispers like they were telling dirty jokes in a church.

As we sat, Loral walked away, speaking to someone behind a desk, and I thought it was important to memorize the way the rooms attention followed every shift in her posture. They gravitated around her, almost desperate to keep her in view. I wasn't sure I could pretend to be in such awe of someone, but there might be a time I'd have to try.

"Seems a little too comfortable here," I said nervously. I felt my body relax immediately as it hit the pillows, practically leeching out any tension or stress. I could tell Victor and Catherine felt the same sensation, but was surprised by the disgust twisting Victor's lips.

"This really is some cruel game they are playing," Victor mumbled, closing his eyes while his head dropped back. He jolted back up for a second and then his head fell back again.

"What do you mean?" I whispered.

"Our eyes. It's like they are mocking us by taking them away." Images of Victor Herse's murder scenes flashed in my mind. I'd never understood why he only took the right eye of his victims before killing them, but by the tone in his voice it was borderline blaspheme. "This type of weird is out of my league. I don't know about you, Jared," he yawned, "but if there's another door I want to find it now."

"This place..." Catherine breathed slowly. "This is what the voices promised if I didn't help you."

"Promised?" I said rubbing my eyes, tiredly.

"Peace. They promised…peace."

Looking half drugged, Victor slid off his backpack and crawled a few feet, stuffing it against the wall. "Something's…wrong….," he mumbled. "I can't…stay awake. Don't let them get this bag, Jared. Whatever you do…"

The pillows were heavenly. I heard Victor's mumbling about traps before he seemed to fall dead on his face, but I didn't care, all I wanted to do was slip away in comfort. After days with the vipers, the idea of relaxation was tantalizing. The questions swirling in my head were still there, but they weren't important right now. What came into mind instead was a memory of Kara jamming out and singing Karaoke in her room after I got home late from work one day. She was so full of life; popular, smart, almost too active to keep up with, but more importantly she always knew how to relax me. I watched her in her element for ten minutes before she saw me and screamed, but moments like that always reminded me of why I was a cop. Protecting peace, giving people a chance to be happy…

I woke up, annoyed that I couldn't remember falling asleep. Victor and Catherine were gone, along with the other two strangers. My head felt cloudy, and it took me a few moments to notice that someone was rubbing my back. My hand shot up, grabbing the intruder as I twisted around.

I barely recognized the young woman that knelt behind me as the same terrified girl I'd seen earlier. She'd been beautified with golden flowing hair, lipstick, and earrings, but without eyes and bloody tears I would have easily mistaken her except for the small bandage on her neck.

"You're okay?" I said surprised, releasing her hand from my grip.

The girl's expression never changed as she used her hands to guide me to a forward facing position. I probably looked like a frightened teenager as her hands began to glide softly over my shoulders and across my neck.

"What happened to you?" I whispered.

The only response I received was a gentle shush, like I was being put down for nap.

"Did they drug us? Where are my friends?"

She gave me another shush, and slapped my shoulder playfully.

The silent massage went on for fifteen minutes, and it felt like a ticking time bomb was going off in my mind. No one else in the room acted as if anything was out of the ordinary, and the girl never spoke a word. I had to admit it was fantastic, probably the best I'd ever had, but I needed to focus on how to get out of here. I'd blown my chance to talk to Victor and Catherine, to see if they knew something about this place that I didn't. Hotel Saint's Tower seemed harmless, but it was still the Tower.

"I figured you for the type that would like proof that the girl was safe," Loral said with a smile as she stepped down the stairs. "I have already shown the others to their rooms, would you like to see yours now?"

"Okay," I said a bit dazed. "You have any coffee? I need to wake up."

"I suspect there will be some waiting for us. Follow me. You must have been exhausted to fall asleep for so long."

"How long—"

"About four hours. How do you like it here so far?" Loral asked as I trailed after her.

"It's been…strange," I said slowly, choosing the truthful answer in hope that I might stir up a conversation.

"That is typical at first," Loral said casually. "I'm sure you have many questions. You may ask one right now if you please."

I stopped for a second at the bottom of a staircase. I hadn't been ready for that response, and I had to think fast before I missed the opportunity. Direct inquiries about the tower or asking questions that I should already know would lead to suspicion. That left me with only the new stuff I'd seen since being here.

I'm sure I failed miserably, but I summoned up as much meekness as I could and asked. "Why does no one have eyes?"

Her rich laugh caught me by surprise, and she turned to look down the stairs at me. "You can still see can you not?" she asked.

I nodded.

"And you can still feel your eyes, correct?" I nodded again, this time moving my eyes around deliberately. "The eyes are still there, they are merely hidden because you do not truly know the others, just as many do not know you. The eyes are the windows to the deepest part of a person. Once you understand them you will see them."

"What about you?" I asked. "Can you see my eyes?"

"I can see everyone," she said. "You are Jared Reign; skeptical, dangerous, brave, and rash. I know you are hurting deeply, troubled by loss, vulnerable. You value others more than yourself, and you hate with just as much passion as you love. And yet there is more to you than even I can see—as if you have no plan. That concerns me. You had no path before you so you came to us."

I felt exposed, my fight or flight response kicking in, fearing that her generalizations might catch onto the fact that I wasn't here on friendly terms.

"Why are you here, Jared Reign?" She asked dangerously. "Your intentions may be unfocused, but they are sinister."

I felt my anger stir, quickly pushing back sense, but I reined it in just enough to say, "I want answers about this place. None of this makes sense."

I wanted to take that last part back. The voices had seemed to provide Catherine with at least some answers, and if I was missing those answers…

"You were told to have faith, without faith you could not be here," Loral said, "You listened and followed. You have found this place of peace, and now you are shaken?"

I shrugged, hoping for a miracle. "Like you said, skeptical."

"Indeed," Loral said, her eyes thinning before perking up. "I've had bigger challenges though. Come, your room is on the third floor."

I let out a mental deep breath and followed, half expecting her to turn around and reveal that I'd killed her sister.

My room turned out to be a luxury suite. The king size bed was draped with white sheets, the walls were decorated with beautiful rendition paintings and photos, and its wide double balcony doors were left open, letting in a slight breeze that brought with it the smell of summer. The floor was tiled in a white glossy finished marble, using the natural sunlight to brighten the room. There were no electronics or people, leaving only the lengthy lounge couch and sturdy oak table to welcome me in. My throat burned and my stomach growl as I noticed the pitcher of ice water and a basket of bright red apples perched on the table.

"Make this place your home however you like. There is a shower through the door to your right. I'm not sure how you got so grungy, but I suggest you get cleaned up. Your first assignment can begin as early as tomorrow morning if you wish. Someone will show you the way."

"Assignment?" I asked as I walked over to the table and poured myself a glass of water.

Loral looked surprised. "While you are more than welcome to remain here as long as you wish, I was under the impression you were interested in leaving."

"I am," I said taking a drink.

"Then you must serve."

"How long?"

"Three hundred days."

My throat ignored the ice cold water sliding down it, turning to sandpaper while water sloshed from the glass as my hand tensed. "That's a long time," I said, trying to steady my rising anxiety.

"Trust me," Loral smiled, swaying toward the exit, "It will be over before you know it."

A moment later I was left alone, the sound of a lock sliding in place on the other side my only company.

Chapter 15

The sun died a few hours later, leaving only starlight to fall across the marble floor. My shower had been unbelievable, the stream of hot water against my tired body nearing ecstasy. I had scars in every place where the woman in black had stabbed me, but that was small price to pay for being alive.

Slipping on one of the dozens of pairs of white beach pants tucked inside the dresser, I dropped back on the bed. It was comfortable, almost like lying on a cloud, but I couldn't sleep. It had been ghostly quiet since Loral locked me in my luxurious cage; the time alone allowed my thoughts to twist into a torturous pretzel. I felt that every action I could take led to a dead end. I could break down the door, I could jump from the balcony into the crowds of happy people, or I could wait and *serve*. I'd wanted answers to my family's deaths, but it had grown far more complicated than that. I wasn't any closer to knowing where to focus the hatred burning inside me. The tower had proven to be more than just a building. It was more than just a symbol or an entity to be destroyed, and because of that a recipe for sorrow was brewing. I felt as if I stood over Kelesa and Kara's grave every time I closed my eyes, and each time it was harder not to join them. Loral was right about me not having any path.

I heard the door open, but I didn't move. Footsteps, probably bare, entered the room before shutting the door. I opened my eyes enough to see a woman in white lace gliding toward me like an eager cat. It took me a moment to notice that it was the woman from the park and my personal masseuse, Naomi. When she approached the bed she crawled softly across the sheets before straddling me gently.

"Hi," she whispered, smiling down at me, letting her brown hair fall across her shoulders. I had to admit I barely noticed that she still had no eyes.

"Um, hi" I said slowly.

She ran a hand through my hair. "You looked troubled."

"It's been a long day,"

"I would love to help you with that—if you'll let me." She pushed back locks of hair with one hand which then fell softly across her neck and chest. I felt myself gulp, but grabbed her wrist as she began to pull down a silky strap off her shoulder.

"What are you doing?" I asked, keeping my hold.

"Serving you." Using her free hand she guided mine to her thigh, letting out a gentle sigh as she did.

"Naomi," I said, pulling her closer. "What happened to you earlier? What is this place?"

"Don't worry about that," she said, moving down to whisper in my ear. "Let's enjoy our time first."

I felt my heartbeat rabbit into motion as she started to move her hips, but I grabbed both her arms and held her steady.

"I don't want this," I said shaking my head.

"Yes you do," she said sexily. "If I go they will only send another." I was about to say 'let them try', but Naomi dropped her head down slowly and kissed me. After biting my lip a little she said, "You don't want the others, Jared." Her voice was intense, but not sensual, more like she was warning me of something. "When you've see what I've seen…" She went to kiss me again, but this time I let her, feeling the desperation in her movement.

Still holding her arms I rolled her over next to me and let go. "I'm tired," I said. "But don't leave—you can sleep here."

Her chest was rising up and down rapidly, but she didn't make any effort to argue. "If that is how I can serve you," she said.

I rested my head back on the pillows and rubbed my eyes. *This just got a whole lot more complicated.*

"So this is how you serve?" I whispered without turning my head.

"One of the ways," Naomi said, wrapping the sheets around her legs. "Half and half."

"What do you mean?"

She rolled over so that she was facing me. She was beautiful, but all I could picture now were those bleeding eyes. "We spend half of our day relieving the pressures and stresses of others, and the other half in pleasure and peace."

"For three hundred days?"

"Yes."

"And then what?"

"Why don't you know this," she asked curiously. "Do they not speak to you?"

I froze for a minute, not knowing what to say, but decided on a lie. "They do, I just don't understand them."

"After three hundred days of service we move on."

"Move on where?"

For the first time she frowned. "To see our family."

"You don't believe that." I stated quietly.

She moved closer to me, wrapping her leg around mine and pushing her chest against my arm. "Kiss me," she breathed as she began nuzzling against my neck.

I was about to push her away, but the urgency of her body and the movement of her lips stopped me. "I've seen the truth of this place," she whispered as she planted kisses across my neck. "It's wrong, Jared." I could feel her body shutter against mine as her voice trembled. "Escape this place, go south. Find the witch, she will show you the truth."

"The witch?" I said incredulously. The idea of magic was more then I could take at this moment, but what else did I have? "Can she help me escape this place?" I asked.

She rolled on top of me again, resting her forehead against mine. I felt a tear drop on my chin. "'She can help show you the truth, but I don't know about the door. I ran away after…."

"After what?" I whispered.

"I need you to help me, take me with you—kill me. Just don't make me stay. I shouldn't have run. I was so close…"

There was a single knock at the door and Naomi's fingers trembled as she they ran across her face. I turned to see Loral slip into the room, but

Naomi's lips touched mine and I had to fight my instinct to pull away as Loral walked toward the bed.

As Loral put a hand on Naomi's shoulder the terrified girl whispered. "Don't forget about me, Jared, please."

"My dear, it seems we've made a mistake and put you in the wrong room tonight," Loral said. "Although it appears that you are serving Mr. Reign well."

"I don't mind," I said holding on to Naomi's arm. "We were just getting started."

"Alas, Naomi has already been requested by one of our more senior tenants. If you wish, you can make a request for someone else."

"No thanks," I said casually. "I think I'll just get some sleep for tomorrow."

"Naomi dear," Loral said, "You shouldn't keep Mr. Bari waiting."

Naomi slid her bare feet to the floor and bowed her head to Loral before making a hasty escape for the door.

Loral watched as Naomi left and then turned back to me. "Oh, Jared don't look at me that way, what she did here was because she wished it. That girl is as dedicated as they come. Remember, you only serve if you choose. Peace and happiness can't be found without others, but everyone should be able to find it. We are all equal, we serve and are served. We never force anything upon anyone, and no one is hurried to leave. This place will fulfill any desire for as long as you wish."

"But I can't keep Naomi?" I asked sarcastically, sitting up.

Loral just smirked. "By morning you'll have forgotten all about her."

Chapter 16

I awoke with first light, the smell of cool morning air and the sight of a woman lying next to me. It reminded me of the times I'd traced my fingertips against the naked curves of Kelesa's back as she slept. Of course now it wasn't Kelesa I was looking at. I added the pain of that memory to all the others as my fingers ran across the cool metal of my wedding ring, guilt rearing its ugly head as my eyes traveled to the second woman next to me. Naomi had been a novice when it came to seduction compared to these women. I admit, it felt nice to be wanted, to be desired in such primal passion, but Loral was wrong about me forgetting about Naomi. I remembered her with every kiss they tempted me with, I remembered my wife and daughter with each piece of discarded clothing, and I remembered the tower with every touch. I'm not sure how I managed, but sleep was the only thing we'd agreed on, and I'd be lying if at least part me didn't feel like I'd made a colossal mistake.

There was a small knock on the door as a man in white delivered a tray of coffee. The women rolled over as I slid out of bed, but they didn't show any sign of waking up. I threw on a loose white button up shirt before pouring a cup, but I didn't take a drink. My mind was in passive panic. I stared at the two beautiful women laying in my bed, knowing I wouldn't make it another night without feeling like I'd betrayed Kelesa, but at the same time my mind was telling me to just enjoy it, that I'd been through enough. That thought scared me. At its core I was telling myself to let the tower win. I needed to remember the vipers, the names on the mirrors outside the tower, Victor and Catherine, and all the blind love bestowed upon the object that had killed my family. This glimpse of paradise or whatever Loral wanted to describe it as was just another part of its darker side. Naomi had seen it.

I stood and walked to the door, but as I'd assumed it was locked. That right there should be enough to get me through another night, but it wasn't. I felt my heart speed up at the very thought, but I ignored it and took a moment to sip some coffee.

An hour later, after the two supermodels had joined me for a coffee and another round of giggling and teasing, the same man that had delivered coffee arrived to escort them back to their rooms. Then Beltin showed up straight backed and stiff-necked.

"I was informed you wished to be of service today?" he asked flatly, holding the door open. "If so please follow me." As I followed him down the hall I quickly noticed two things. The first was that my door was the only room with a lock on it, and second was that I saw only men moving around.

"So men serve during the day, women serve at night?" I asked.

"For the most part," he answered back.

"What will I be doing today?" I asked, worried that it was my turn to be sent to someone's bed chamber.

"Some of the women are requesting new men to pleasure them, but we need people on sand."

As we entered the lobby we were greeted by an overly jubilant concierge who escorted us out into the city, handing Beltin several cloth bags.

"Sand?"I asked, noticing that the city looked spotless. *How'd I miss this*, I thought. *Sandstorms that don't leave sand*?

"The sand cleanses the city, but it also leaves behind the fruit we eat. It also provides the names for the mirrors."

That stopped me cold. "You mean the names on the outside of the tower?"

Beltin stopped as well, turning sharply on his heels and glaring at me. "You entered through the doors then?" He was good at keeping his lips flat and his cheeks bored, but in his voice I could sense venom.

"Is there another way?"

His calm mask broke slightly, we'll that was an understatement, his face lit up like a cheerleader whose boyfriend had just flirted with someone else, his lips turning into a devilish sneer. "Obviously," he said snidely. "I just thought I was the only one that made it this far after walking through the door."

Soldier boy was actually jealous, I thought in relief. *He'd probably pop a vein if he'd known about Victor and Catherine.* His reaction confused me though; I'd have to figure out why that was so important to him.

He gave me one last bitter look and then continued walking. "Yes the hallowed names. Bringing joy to others is the general purpose of this utopia, but it may not be the most important. The influx of names has been greater lately, but that doesn't make our duty to help others find this place any less important."

I felt my anger clawing its way out, threatening to explode if it wasn't granted satisfaction right then. This place, these people, they were the ones responsible for putting Kelesa and Kara's names on the tower, essentially destroying everything I lived for.

"What do you mean, 'helps them find this place'?"

"That's for the Master of Mirrors to know."

Beltin wasn't even paying attention. His back was turned. It could be quickly, messy likely, but quick. I finally had something tangible to focus my pain on, to let it loose, stop it from tearing me apart from the inside. But something stopped me from beginning what would have turned into a rampage, only stopping when I'd been killed or captured. Instinct, gut, call it what you would, but I've learned to recognize it over the years. It was illogical as all hell, but it, more than anything, usually got the job done.

"Here," Beltin said, squatting down to pick something up. As he turned I noticed a pristine red apple resting in his hand. "When the sands come, they leave piles of these behind." I need you to go around the city collecting as much fruit as you can fit in these bags. Then deliver them to the market in the park. Don't eat any though—the food is only for those off duty. The market is easy to spot near the bridge—feel free to celebrate there when you are finished at four."

"What about the names?" I asked, barely keeping my voice from a growl.

"They appear in Times Square, you can make your way there if you wish, but the fruit is your priority today." As Beltin handed me the bags I could sense a new hostility grow in him. It was like one of those handshakes that were too hard and too long, but in this case he waited for me to pull the bags from him.

"Don't bother the scribes, Reign," he warned. "They need their concentration. I still think Loral is wrong to give you a chance." With that he dropped the apple in a bag, shouldered his way passed me and turned at the closest corner.

I almost stormed off toward Times, walking nearly half a block before doubling back to haphazardly shovel apples into the bag. As much as I hated it, I had to play the part again, follow orders until I knew my options. Knowing about the names put Naomi's witch on hold. Because at the very least I needed to see how the strange sands brought with them the names of the murdered.

Chapter 17

The apples had grown warm beneath the sun's heat, practically sweating as much as I was. Small beads of perspiration glistened off of their glossy red skin, and if I hadn't just stepped into Times Square my exhaustion and hunger would have blinded me to Beltin's orders.

A reverent silence blanketed the streets of Manhattan's central hub. It felt empty compared to a normal day at the number one tourist spot in the world, but rows of hundreds of people in white sat in the street with their legs folded, each one holding a notepad in their hands while locked in a deep state of meditation. Where there were usually dozens of giant images of soft drinks, cologne ads, theatre promotions, and fast food teasers, there were now depictions of what I could only describe as modern art. The disorganized shapes and colors splattering themselves against the sides of buildings were as stunning as they were overwhelming, but there were no names.

I walked around the crowds, trying to see if there was a hint to what I was missing, but even with as much focus as the scribes were giving the portraits, their notepads were all blank. I let out a faint grunt of disappointment, letting impatience shower me with doubt. I'd thought the grunt was only loud enough for me, but the two men in white next to me seemed to shake out of their trance. Their eyeless glare wasn't angry however, only confused, like they weren't sure where they were. A few seconds later they slipped away again.

Although the majority of the crowd was men, years of marriage to Kelesa must have trained my brain to spot her red hair from anywhere, because my eyes practically zeroed in on one of the few women sitting on the ground. She was on the opposite side of me, but even from a distance I could tell it was Catherine.

I dropped my bags of apples on the sidewalk and used my practice against the vipers to move silently across the street. There were three people between me and Catherine, but I threw caution to the wind and stepped across the strangers, sitting down in the space between. The others looked at me dreamily as our shoulders hit, but their attention drifted slowly back toward the buildings.

I crossed my legs and nudged Catherine with my arm. She kinda wobbled a little bit, and it took two more nudges to finally get her to turn. It looked like she had to relearn to use her lips, but eventually she said, "Jared?"

"What's going on here?" I asked, checking to make sure I wasn't catching anyone's attention. "What's happened to you since we got separated?"

Her checks flushed red, and she looked away. "I'm looking for a name."

"Why?" I asked. "How?"

"It's hard to explain," she whispered. "I'm not even sure it was explained right to me, but if you focus hard enough the meaning of the picture will tell you the name."

My eyes drifted to the chaotic splatter paint, and I could feel it tug at my attention. "Then what?"

"We write the name down, and give it to that man over there." Catherine pointed toward a short man kneeling at the base of the One Times Square building. He had long white hair, but didn't look old. He was a lanky man with a dimpled chin, and his round rimmed sun-glasses made him look more human than everyone else around me. "They call him The Master of Mirrors. If we give him a name we are done for the day….." Catherine's voice trailed off, "Jared…are you okay?"

I wasn't okay, but I didn't say it. Instead, I watched the noon day sun reflect its light off the two mirrors that sat directly in front of The Master of Mirrors. It seemed absurd that those could be connected to the same mirrors on the door to the tower, but there was no other explanation. I was now seeing proof that the tower was responsible for killing my wife and daughter.

Protocol, I always hated the word, complicated investigations more than anything else, but in most cases it kept the criminal from escaping on a technicality. Protocol dictated that you needed both evidence and motive before convicting someone of a crime, and while protocol had no room here, I couldn't help but run it through my mind. I set out to prove to myself and the world that we'd been toyed with, that even Saints Tower's name was a lie; I came to reap vengeance for what it took from me though truth, but I'd hit a brick wall. I might as well have been making a case to throw a car into prison. The tower wasn't a person, and clearly it didn't follow the same rules as everyone else. My eyes narrowed on the lanky man guarding the mirrors, and I suddenly had an idea.

I'd run into those that seemed untouchable by the law, corporation's or crime bosses whose money and influence had more power than any precinct. I had to treat the tower the same, and target the grunts of the operation, bring it down from within. Besides, I'd already started with the woman in black.

Part of me wanted to finish the Master of Mirrors, take him out for what he was responsible for, but first I had to grasp the chance to find the true purpose behind the names, find the towers motive and exploit it. The Master of Mirrors would lead me to answers.

I'd seen the result of not seeing knowing the true motive of people, it was one reason catching Victor Herse had been so difficult, but there was another mistake that would make me hesitate for the rest of my life. The only memory fresher was getting the call that my wife and daughter had been in a car accident.

We call it failure when it takes four months to understand a killer's pattern, and a disaster when you end up face to face with said killer alone. Sirens blared in the distance of the dark city, but it was clear that backup wasn't going to make it in time to stop Jack Stiv. He had the family—a wife and two kids—gagged and bound in the bedroom, but his shotgun hovered mere inches from the bruised and beaten man in the next room.

"You hear that?" I barked out, taking a few steps forward as I aimed the barrel of my Glock toward Jack. "Every cop in the city knows where you are. Just drop the weapon and it will all be over. You've left enough families fatherless already."

"I'm not finished," Jack screamed, stabbing the barrel of the gun into the man's head.

"We know what happened, Jack," I said calmly. "Your family is safe, we found them."

I could tell the news shocked Jack, but it wasn't enough to distract him. "That's impossible," he said shaking. "I saw the video. They killed them. I had to watch!"

"It was a lie, Jack. They weren't killers, just cowards. When you didn't pay them the ransom, they panicked. The video was staged to buy them time. Trent here told us their location after we warned him you were coming after him."

Jack's eyes narrowed. "Oh, I'm not after him. He's the one that shot them. He's the one killed my family. He's the one that gets to suffer! Now he gets to watch!"

As Jack's eyes traveled to the bedroom, I saw the small remote control in his right hand. It was too late, but I pulled the Glock's trigger. I saw the bullet hit his chest. It should have been enough, but before I could see the second shot hit, I was thrown across the room as the bedroom buckled and shattered under the pressure of the explosion.

I felt my hands shaking as I stared at the man in the sunglasses. I couldn't make that mistake again. This man could easily have been responsible for what happened to Kelesa and Kara, but there was always the chance I was wrong, and like with Jack, sometimes being wrong came at too big a price.

If the names were really meant to better the lives of the others outside than I needed to understand what went wrong, and if the intention of the names was corrupted from the start I needed to find out why.

"Jared," Catherine asked. "What's going on?"

I peeled my eyes away long enough to see Catherine's worried face. "I need you tell me what you think of this place. What side are you on?"

"What do you mean?" she asked.

"You came into this tower looking for your son, but when you heard the voices, despite thinking you were going crazy you listened. And now you're kneeling in the middle of a street following the orders of people you've never met before, and you seem happy about it even though your boyfriend was torn to pieces a day or two ago. I plan on taking this tower down. Tell me, Catherine, what do you plan on doing?"

My bluntness seemed to knock life back into her, but she didn't say anything. "Alright I'm leaving," I said standing.

"Wait," she said quickly grabbing my arm. I could sense the calm of the crowd around us beginning to break as more and more faces turned our way, so I sat down. "I…I don't know what to do. This place is strange, Jared, but it makes me feel welcome. They said the first place was a test, and now we get to do our part to be happy and to make others happy. They say I get to be with my family if I am faithful."

"You mean the voices say?"

Catherine's lips tightened. "Yes."

"And you believe them?"

"What other choice do I have?"

I started to say something but then I closed my mouth. I really didn't know what else to offer her. I knew what I needed to find, but I wasn't sure how I was going to, or how long it was going to take, or what I was going to do when I found it. Besides, if something was offering me Kelesa and Kara back, I'd probably take it.

I took a deep breath. "If I find another choice, are you willing to go against the tower?"

It took her awhile, but then Catherine nodded. "It killed Blake."

Just then a man a few rows away stood, holding his notepad high in the air. The Master of Mirrors perked up, but didn't turn around. Standing from his kneeling position he moved toward the mirrors and rang a light bell that signaled another man into the crowd to retrieve the notepad. A minute later the Master of Mirrors stared down at the notepad as the man held it up. His smile sharpened as if the piece of paper was a precious diamond, his greed evident in the way he licked his lips.

And then he did something unexpected. Rolling out a cart that was set next to the mirrors, he took a strange looking pen and began etching the name onto his forearm. When he was done he walked over to the mirrors, and in a drawn out motion, shoved his right arm through the right mirror. Then, in a cry of ecstasy his arm slid back out, washing the name 'Wendy Carmichael' from his arm and leaving the name emblazoned in reverse within the mirror.

Images of the same scene, only with Kelesa and Kara's name etched onto the man's arms, played through my mind. It was strange sure, but knowing that it had been so simple made it hurt even more. How did *that* lead to their deaths, or to the good luck it gave everyone else? I should have been use to unexplainable events happening by now, but seeing the man's arm go through the glass like that made my stomach clench. I wasn't good with weird. I tangled with some messed up people in my career, but it had always somehow made sense. I ran a hand through my hair and sighed. *Everyone but Victor.*

I felt I knew more about Victor than anyone else, but I could never explain his actions with logic. I merely knew how he would react. If anyone could understand the Master of Mirrors it would be him.

"I need to go," I whispered to Catherine. "I'll find you when I know what to do next."

"Be careful," Catherine said as she stared toward the mirrors. "They are getting suspicious."

Chapter 18

The market had to be the most frightening place I'd seen yet, and by frightening I meant groups of men and women laughing and playing like little children, giggling and teasing each other as if it were morning recess. The area surrounding the iconic bridge of Central Park had become home to a giant half farmers market, half fair. People sunbathed, absorbing the mild heat waves, while other sat in small groups, enjoying picnic baskets of fresh fruit. The whole scene would have made me uncomfortable—I being more at ease in confusing chaos apparently—but my desire for a big steak was growing exponentially. I'd seen so much fruit on my way back from Times Square that I didn't even want to sneak a bite. *Half and half,* I thought. *I've done the work; the least they can do is feed me something savory.*

Hefting the bags of fruit onto the wooden market stall, I received an enormous smile from the man on the other side.

"You're a half hour late, Jared" the man said.

"Putting in some overtime," I said back distracted. My mind was busy trying to figure out where Victor could be.

The confusion on the man's face was classic. "I don't think we do overtime."

I shrugged. "First day—you know."

"Ah, a newcomer," he cheered. "Feel free to join the festivities. Eat as much as you like!"

"I think I'll just head back to my room," I paused for a moment, realizing for the first time that the man knew my name. "Any chance you know where my friend Victor Herse is hiding." I tried to say 'friend' as genuinely as possible, but the man noticed my undertone.

I sensed the lie coming before he even opened his lips. "No idea," he said flatly.

"Oh well, he's probably finishing his *service*."

The man's lip twitched, but he didn't say anything. His silence told me more than I needed. Victor had skipped out on the service portion of this trip.

"Thanks," I said, wiping beads of sweat off my forehead. How did everyone else tolerate this heat?

I turned to head back to the hotel, but only made it ten feet before Loral stepped from behind a tree and in front of me. I wasn't proud of it, but I jumped. After a life time of seeing people with eyes I wasn't overly shocked that my thoughts shouted 'freak!'

"I was looking for you," I said quickly, thinking on my feet.

"Oh. What for darling? For a moment there you looked startled."

"I was hoping you could send some more girls over tonight—say, around midnight."

Her smile beamed. "Ah, I see you've grasped how we do things around here. But I'm afraid I have to decline this time."

"How come?" I said, trying to sound disappointed.

She moved closer, swaying her hips until she pressed against my chest and stood on tip toe. Her lips brushed slightly against mine and my whole body shivered with pleasure. "I've decide I'll join you tonight."

"Wh—why?" I cleared my throat. "Why do I deserve that?"

"You intrigue me, Jared Reign. I want to get to know you better. Besides, you are quite striking." She walked behind me, her hand running across my chest until she was out of view. "I hope collecting fruit didn't sap too much of your strength."

Crap, I thought as I tried to slow my heartbeat. *It's never good to attract the attention of the queen.*

I practically ran to the hotel when Loral was out of sight, feeling the door of an invisible iron maiden closing in on me. I caught my breath before approaching the concierge, but then changed my mind and just headed to the staircase. Asking about Victor again would probably be like tying the rope around my neck. I skipped the second and third floor, climbing until I got to the fourth. My hope was that Victor's door had a lock like mine, but the third and fourth floors were all open cages. It wasn't until the sixth floor that I found another door with a lock.

Long behold, the door didn't budge. I grabbed the frame with both arms and rested my head on the door tiredly. Catherine's warning told me I had to be careful, but Loral's attention meant I was out of time. I wasn't sure what that implied entirely, but I didn't want to find out. I took a deep breath, decided that the time for play-acting and subtly was over, and kicked in the door.

I'd picked the right room. I saw Victor. I saw the blood. And I saw the victims. I hated being right.

Chapter 19

It was difficult to tell that the bed sheets were once white. The room was bright, sunlight making the blood caking the bed seem like a rose pattern. Broken breathing and muffled sobs were heavy in the room, almost like they were masks for the screams that should have been coming from the three women collapsed against the wall.

No matter how many crime scenes I'd witnessed it was always a challenge not to look away, but this time I did. I grasped the door frame, afraid my knees would give out. Usually I had time to prepare for this—a trip across town, a phone call warning me of what I was about to see. Never had the murder still been in progress.

Victor straddled the woman on the bed, his knife pressed against her temple as his eyeless gaze stared at me. Was he surprised? Annoyed? Without his eyes I had no idea.

I stared back for a moment, unsure what to do, but when Victor turned back to the woman and pushed the knife into her flesh I grabbed the first thing I could find. I hurled the four legged chair at him, knocking the serial killer to the floor.

"Herse!" I screamed, running around the bed. He stood frantically, hands in the air, holding something that made my stomach churn. My vision flickered back to the woman then back to Victor's hand, struggling to except the reality that her eye wasn't were it was supposed to be. Where there was nothing before, the woman's eye socket was now bare, bleeding onto the pillow that her head was resting on. My eyes shot to the other three women against the wall, and that's when I lost it.

I charged Victor Herse, tackling him against the wall, his head creating a solid thump as it dented the sheet rock. I'd meant to punch him, but an overwhelming sense of nausea hit and I fell against him. I elbowed him in the face before he rolled away, but he climbed to his feet, jumping over the bed and the woman.

"Stop," Victor whispered desperately, after spitting out blood. "I can explain this." I made a move to swing around the bed, but the fact that he was whispering slowed me. "There's this woman," he said quickly. "They call her the witch. I went to see her."

"That doesn't change the fact that you just killed four people," I growled loudly.

"Keep it down you idiot," he whispered again. "I know what this looks like. In your position and with our history, it's a no brainer. If it makes you feel better I won't kill them, but I think that's a bad idea. I can't help them embrace anything at this point."

"What are you talking about?" *Breathing*, my brain pointed out. *They are all still breathing.*

"There is something wrong with these people, Jared. It's like they are empty. Ending this existence for them means nothing."

"So you cut out their eyes!" I shouted incredulously.

"I need them," he whispered. "We need them. It's the only way we can justly see. The witch's words, not mine."

"I can't accept this," I said breathing quickly. "This is wrong."

"What are you gonna do, Jared. Kill me? Turn me in to Loral? This is all we got. Get it together or we're screwed."

Victor was covered in blood, his loose white shirt lost beneath the pain and violence he caused. The eyeball dangling from his hand was revolting, the room was a psychological nightmare, and yet the stench of death was missing. Victor was a murderer, he was mad, he killed for unexplainable reasons, and yet this time he hadn't.

I had two conflicting hatreds for this man. The first was that I had no way to bring him to justice for any of this, and the second was that I couldn't understand this tower, but he could. I wasn't sure what was real, what was illusion, what was sane; I'd lost all grasp on reality. I was hunting for the motive behind my family's killers, trying to find reason behind their deaths, but what if there wasn't a reason. All sense said there probably wasn't a motive—that crap just happened. That maybe Benjamin was right and it really was just an accident. I'd gained too much negative attention in this bizzaro Manhattan; my last act could easily be taking out the madman in front of me—take him out of this world so he couldn't hurt more people—but instead I just stood there.

"Truth," I heard Kelesa's voice whisper in my mind. "If there is ever a high price to pay, it's always for the truth." It was something she told me when we'd first met after I'd joked about her wanting to marry a detective. It was a hard life, but she respected it.

"Jared?" Victor whispered, still not moving. "You okay in there?"

"If you are lying about these girls, Herse," I said trembling with rage, "I'll end you."

"They'll be fine, I promise," Victor said. "Does that mean we are a team again?"

I just glared at him.

"We need to leave, now, but there is one thing," Victor said holding up a finger. He moved over toward the ice bucket on the table and sat the eye he was holding inside. "Two each," he said, tilting the bucket so I could see. "Don't ever say I didn't think of you."

I gagged, feeling a bit of my soul self destructed. *What was I doing?*

Victor grabbed his backpack off of a chair and walked onto the balcony, looking down. "Last time I spent an hour climbing down the wall, but you did just break down the door... I said I wanted the girls all evening, so if you're brutish actions didn't draw too much attention we can just slip—" Victor stopped and turned around slowly, probably sensing the same wave of danger I did.

A second later I heard the distinct sound of a pump action shot gun being primed.

The barrel swung around the corner of the door first, giving me just enough time to dive behind the bed as the round peppered the wall with holes and murdered the feather pillows. I took a second to peek over the edge of the bed as I heard the next pump. Beltin strolled into the room like the terminator with Loral right behind him. The next shot was at Victor, the round shattering the glass of the balcony window. Victor ducked around the side out of view, holding the bucket of eyes against his chest.

"Throw me a pillow case,' Victor whispered.

"I knew you would be trouble!" Loral screamed as my hands stumbled across the floor. I didn't know what good a pillow case would do, but when I found one I tossed it in front of the door. "I tried to welcome you into my family, and this is how you betray me!? How dare you desecrate my children! Kill them, Beltin!! Kill them!"

Victor's hand shot around the door frame a half second before the next shot blew the wall into pieces. Victor stumbled from cover, hissing. "I was really hoping I wouldn't have to use plan c,' he said, grabbing the balcony's railing for support. As the next shot fell into the chamber, Victor dumped the bucket into the pillow case and jumped. The scattershot clanged against the metal of the railing just as Victor's head disappeared from view.

"Get the other one!" Loral screamed.

As Beltin stepped into view I felt the bed move behind me. A moment later Loral's hands grasped my skull, squeezing with supernatural strength. Beltin's shotgun was aimed at my chest as I tried to fight her off, but my main concern was that my head was going to crack under the pressure. "Now," Loral ordered. "Shoot now!"

My guttural scream must have covered up the fact that Naomi had entered the room, because Beltin never saw the glass pitcher that she swung at his head. In an act of desperation my hands reached back, searching Loral's face until they felt where her eyes should be. As my thumbs pressed into her sockets my vision turned red as blood began flowing back through my head. Loral screamed as I crawled away gasping for breath.

"Get out of here," Naomi said as she helped me up. "Don't worry about—"

The butt of Beltin's shotgun found the back of her head. In a fit a rage, or delirium, I wasn't sure which, I grabbed Beltin's shotgun, pushed it against his chest, and tackled him into the wall. The attack barely fazed him, and he shoved back, sending me sliding back against the floor like a child.

I had only a moment to see Naomi's lifeless body on the floor before Beltin took aim, but as I sprinted toward the balcony and jumped over the ledge, I felt I knew Naomi. She was a fighter, a survivor, and her eyes were jade—not blue.

Chapter 20

My arms flailed wildly on the way down, keen to the knowledge that I was going to die. It only took a few seconds to see what Victor's plan c was, but it wasn't a good one. The clear blue of the swimming pool approached faster than a freight train as the people below swam away in panic.

I managed to straighten my body at the last second, but the impact still rattled my brain and played break the wish bone with my body. At that speed I might as well have been hitting cement, but somehow my body listened when I told it to swim up.

A year later, when my head broke the surface, I gasped for air as water ran through my vision. The people in the pool were all gawking at me, but some of them were looking toward the edge of the pool were Victor was climbing out. I swam toward him, following the trail of red that he left in his wake.

"Plan C?" I groaned as I crawled onto the ground next to Victor.

"I'm just happy we hit the deep end," Victor said, checking inside his pillow case.

"You didn't know?"

"Didn't have time. Look the ice is already melting. We need to get moving."

"You're shot," I said standing.

"Just nicked me," Victor said walking toward the exit. "Might have a piece of metal somewhere, but I can deal with it. Seriously, who misses with a shotgun?"

"Where are we going?" I asked once we were on the street.

"Southwest, towards Hell's Kitchen. The witch is bunkered up down there."

It didn't take long for our clothes to dry under the sun, and Victor used his pillow case to cover up the bloodstains on his right hip. Soon we were just another couple of happy white cultist walking down the street. I tried to ignore the guilt I felt about Naomi and the other women as we moved with the crowds, but when did guilt ever really fade? I was taught from childhood to avoid doing things I'd feel guilty about. It was good advice—but never really felt possible.

I was almost grateful for the distraction when our moment of calm came to an abrupt halt. I mean it literally came to a halt. Everyone on the street stopped moving at the same time. I stopped with the crowd, my momentum only bumping a few people ahead of me I was ready to apologize, but then every eyeless face in the city turned toward me. I stopped breathing. I knew that dreamy look—I'd seen it on Catherine's face multiple times now. Like the flip of a switch, the voices were giving the orders now.

Victor must have seen it coming as well, because neither one of us hesitated to bull over everyone and break into a dead sprint.

They weren't crazed, they weren't even angry, but just the same the whole city had suddenly become a mob of dangerous killers. The determination on their faces as they chased was scary. Some threw rocks or food, others found sticks and knives.

When I'd first join the force when I was twenty, I'd had to deal with a riot. It had given me valuable insight on how creative people could be when they weren't thinking. This was worse. I ran all out, but there were ambushes on every next corner. Clusters of people stormed out of subway exits, the buildings looked like ant farms as people tunneled through revolving doors.

My right calf got hit with a brick, my forearm was bruised from stopping a baseball bat, but somehow we kept moving, barely staying ahead of the swarm behind us.

"Still think I was wrong about those women!" Victor shouted as we wrestled off a man that had just jumped out of a two story window on top of us.

I pulled out a piece of glass from the back of my hand as we continued to run. "Shut up!" I shouted.

"Here!" Victor said, pointing toward a fire station. "She's in there." Victor pulled open the red door and ran inside, slamming it shut after I'd followed.

The door buckled under the onslaught outside, threatening to snap off its rusty hinges as Victor fumbled to slide a heavy metal bar into place. And then suddenly silence consumed everything. Blackness snuffed out the line of light beneath the door and the barrage of screams and shouts on the other side were deafened.

"Where'd they go?" I panted.

It was dark and quiet, a nightmare of absence. Instinctively, I tried to control wild breathing, but it only forced my heartbeat to race until it was thundering in my skull. I heard Victor try the same, his long drawn breaths escaping in short gasps. As my eyes adjusted, the darkness began carrying a red tint, outlining the shape of a single downward staircase.

Without warning a hand grasped my shoulder, its skin barely clinging to the long thin bones beneath. I jumped at the vile contact, spinning defensively as my back slammed against the door.

"I've bought us sometime to… chat," a gravelly voice said.

I opened my mouth to respond, but nothing came out as I watched a flame flicker to life and move toward the crown of the stairs. An ancient woman, probably four feet tall, withered so much she barely looked human, beckoned me toward her with one long crooked finger. I felt my stomach churn at her appearance. Two torn pieces of cloth covered her chest and groin, leaving her nearly fleshless rib cage exposed. Her nose was deflated, pressed flatly against her face, and her head was bald except for a few wisps of grey. Sunken, hollowed eye sockets stared back at me as her one toothed grin welcomed me to hell.

"I do love visitors," she said hoarsely. "Oooo, and you brought me presents. I can smell them."

Chapter 21

My footsteps echoed in the blackness as we sunk below, guided by a speck of light and a damp, jagged rail. Sounds of metal scrapping and rats skittering whispered from the deep. A rotten stench, a mix of road kill and iron, grew stronger with each step. Down, I felt, was the worst place to follow a strange old lady.

Eventually the bottom of the stairs opened up into a dark room, the kind where film was developed back in the day. I staggered, wishing my eyes would shut. Instead, they took in the blood smeared floor, the rusted knives and tools that sat haphazardly against dissected corpses, and the spilt metal buckets of... I turned and threw up, adding to the vileness of the demonic morgue. I'd seen some pretty horrible things in my career, some nearly as bad as this, but my stomach refused to keep calm.

"Good, good," the witch said moving toward a set of chairs. "Get it out now detective. Consider this practice."

"What's that supposed to mean?" I said, whipping stomach acid from my lips.

"Take a seat," she croaked, ignoring my question. "Take a seat and we can talk."

Two stained wooden chairs sat near the back side of the room next to what appeared to be an old fashioned film projector. Behind that sat the refrigeration units where dead human beings hung like discarded waste, limbs and faces sticking out in distorted ways. I d seen many morgues in my life, it was part of most murder investigations, but this one was twisted.

"I can't do this," I said shaking my head and turning for the stairs. "I don't even know how I let it get this far. I must...I must..." I felt dizzy, unable to focus on any one thing as I walked into the wall like a ragdoll.

"Yes you do," The witch screamed, the ghastly sound tightening my spine to the point of snapping. I took a sharp breath, and for a moment I was sure my body had decided it was over, refusing to exhale for what felt like a minute. "You're here because your wife was murdered!" The witch snarled, again moving toward me in a rage, drool splashing from her mouth. "It's in your nature to find out who and why!"

"The cost for this one it to high," I whimpered, leaning away from the woman into the cold wall.

"The cost of truth is always high?" The witch said.

"Then tell me!" I shouted, balling my fists, finally finding the strength to stand back up. "Tell me what truth is worth ignoring all this insanity for! Victor cut out those woman's eyes! You have dead bodies two feet away from you. I was ready to die for the truth—"

"But now you can't die," she shouted, cutting me off. The witch's face turned into a frown, and despite the ugliness I could see real empathy as her dead skin touched my face. "You feel responsible, just like you did after your family died."

"I let it happen," I looked at the room again and shuddered. "I should stop this, just like I should have…" I growled, "I don't see how."

"I know," the witch said sadly. "But you do your best. In your career, there have been times where you let a thief free in order to catch a murderer, or you cut a deal with a drug dealer to find the supplier. This is no different."

"Then who is the supplier?" I asked.

"I can't tell you that."

"Why not?!" I felt my anger rising again, but something told me that was exactly what the witch had intended, so I held back.

"I can only show you the way down."

"Down?" Victor chimed in.

"You must go down before you can go up," the witch crackled impatiently.

"What's the point?" I said. "I don't understand any of this."

"That's what the eyes are for. That's why I asked Victor to do such a vile task. You would not have done so, but you need the eyes to find the way."

A single pair of jade eyes came into focus in my mind, and I stared at the witch as I walked back in the room. "Naomi came here. She told me she'd seen the truth. Did she have to cut out eyes as well?"

"Yes," the witch said casually, walking to one of the dead bodies. "Naomi… much like you, grew desperate enough to ask me for help. This man here was her victim. She wasn't as proficient at retrieval as Victor. It ended poorly."

"Skills are skills," Victor shrugged. "Wish I had a camera right now, Reign. You're reminding me of a little girl."

"Victor Herse!" the witch pronounced coldly. Bony fingers curled around a heavy kitchen knife and flashed toward Victor. "I want you to image for one second that this body here is Amber's. Go on, you're creative." Victor gasped for a moment as he looked at the body, his lips dropping open in wonder. In a speed I wouldn't have expected from the old lady she stabbed the knife into the skull of the corpse. Slowly she began carving into it. Victor jumped up, his body shaking as his eyes grew wide. For a moment his hands pretended to grasp the old ladies throat, but then his face went pale and his face looked dumbfounded.

"That is how a *normal* person feels when they see a dead body."

"How did you…" Victor stammered.

"Just because their minds don't work like yours, doesn't mean they are wrong. But I suspect you've already realized that."

"Touché," Victor growled, taking a seat. "Don't mean I wasn't right before. And if you ever do that again…"

"Take a seat, Detective Reign," the witch urged, ignoring Victor's threat. "Our time is growing short."

Reluctantly, I sat in the wooden chair next to Victor, feeling like a student in a haunted asylums version of medical school. The witch moved into the shadows behind us out of view, and I heard a faint click, followed by an electric buzz that filled the room.

I shielded my eyes against the sudden explosion of grainy white light blinking from the film projector. A few seconds later an unstable picture of the Saints Tower appeared, its name splashed across the top in slanted black lettering.

"This is where you are, correct?" The witch asked tiredly.

"You tell us," Victor said annoyed.

"How did you get here?" she asked acidly.

"What's the point of this?" Victor said standing. "We came through the door."

The witch shook her head impatiently at Victor like he was a misbehaving student and pointed at the chair. As he sat back down, the slide show changed to a choppy mug shot of Victor, then to a mug shot of me. "What did you do the day before you came into the tower?"

I felt my irritation growing, I wanted answers not questions. "I was at a funeral," I mumbled.

"Victor?"

Victor's jaw set in a straight line as he watched the projector transition into a wide view angle of central park and the tower. "I visited Amber's burial site... with her daughter."

"Both journeys began where others ended, but why?" The witch rasped, coughing loudly.

The image on the screen changed again, showing Kelesa and Kara Reign etched on the mirrors of the tower doors, then they flickered to Amber Birch.

"Names," I spat out, perking up slightly. I'd nearly forgotten all about the scribes since walking in on Victor. "I saw where they come from, but I didn't understand it."

"It's because you don't look back far enough."

"You know where they... you didn't tell me?" Victor sputtered.

"We were busy," I said quickly. "What do you mean witch?"

"My name is Linva," the witch said offended. "Tell me Detective Reign. How is it that you don't know what your wife was doing the day before her name appeared on the tower?"

I started to say something, but my mouth just hung open dumbfounded. I'd never thought about it. I should have thought about it. I remembered I was working. Kelesa had a conference to go to in the city. I dropped her off on the way." It was all coming in pieces, but nothing was standing out.

"Watch," the witch said as the projector changed. The Wise Ones stood in front of a crowd seemingly trying to calm them. "Who is responsible for this?' The Buddhist woman called out when silence was finally achieved. "Come on, who?"

It took a moment before the crowd parted, but when it did it revealed a short brunette girl. She was probably fifteen at the most, skinny with a freckled nose. Her blue t-shirt was stained with tears, and she looked terrified.

The Wise Ones looked stunned, shifting uneasy as they took the girl in. "You did this?"

The girl nodded, pulling the spray can out from behind her back. The camera swung around to show four distinctive letters crudely written on the base of the tower. The word 'EVIL' dripped in blood red paint, horrifying everyone around it.

"Why?" the priest asked.

"It lied to my mom," the girl sobbed. "It said she'd be happy, but now she's gone."

"My dear child," the Arab wise man said kneeling. "Moving on is sometimes what makes us happy."

The girls eyes grew wide and she hurled the paint can at the wise ones. "The towers supposed to help people!" she screamed. "Not let them drown!"

The Buddhist woman was motioning toward the girl, signaling the police that had just arrived. The policeman looked at the vandalism and then towards the girl and frowned. "You'll have to come with me," he said, pulling out his handcuffs and moving toward the girl.

The girl was trembling as the cop moved forward, but just before he was about to a haul her away someone's shout broke the silence. "Stop!"

I felt my heart seize up as Kelesa and Kara stepped in front of the little girl, Kelesa's right hand stretched out to bar the cop as the other held on to Kara. "She just a girl," Kelesa said. "She's lost her mom. Who here wouldn't react like this if the promises they were given were taken away."

The cop stopped and looked at Kelesa guiltily. "This isn't the first time, Ma'am."

Kelesa looked at the girl and smiled. Then she turned and did something I'd seen her do many times. She stood tall, locking eyes with each person in the crowd for moment and said, "Her only crime is giving any credit to that thing." Kelesa pointed at the tower, where the paint on the side was already fading. The crowd gasped, recoiling at the accusing tone Kelesa had used. It didn't take long for them to start another round of accusations and chaos, but Kelesa just stood there calmly until it died down.

Kara walked over to the girl and put her arm around her shoulder. "It'll be okay. My dad used to be a cop, he'll fix everything."

"Listen to what this girl has to say," Kelesa said loudly. "A name on the tower doesn't always mean happiness."

"You're just jealous your name hasn't appeared," someone from the crowd shouted.

"Even if it did," Kelesa called back. "My happiness comes from elsewhere."

The movie went silent then, but I watched as the cop spoke to Kelesa a moment before handcuffing the girl and escorting all three of them away. Then, like ripping away a child's sucker, the projector cut out, sputtering to a stop as it began smoking.

I turned to Victor who was looking at me with shock. "What?"

"I know that girl," Victor said slowly. "That was Amber's daughter, Pren."

The name jumped out at me like a fiery serpent. I'd recognized the girl as well. She was the reason we were in the city the day Kelesa and Kara died. Like Kara had said, I'd pulled some strings to get the girl released with no charges, and Pren was the first one that warned me that the tower was going to kill my family.

"Now for the fun part," the witch cackled, opening up the pillowcase that Victor had set aside.

"What was the point of that?" I asked nervously.

The witch pulled the eyes out and examined them. "I suppose green will do, she mumbled before looking up. "The point? The point was to make you think. You're a detective, figure it out."

"Was a detective," I corrected. "I wasn't very good at it."

"That's just insulting," Victor said, holding a hand to his heart. "You did capture me after all."

The witch reached behind one of the metal tables and rustled in what sounded like a bag of metal until she produced what looked like an ice cream scoop.

"You boys want the easy way or the hard way?" The witch said, carelessly pushing the corpses off the table.

"Huh?" I asked. I stood and took a few steps back as she patted the medical table.

"Hard way then," the witch said reaching behind the table again. At first I thought she'd pulled a gun on me, but when there was no bang as she pulled the trigger I only had a second to realize I was wrong. I shook to the ground, the taser gun blitzing all my nerves into overload. I felt dread cloud my mind and I could only focus enough to hear the dull clunk of Victor landing next to me.

"It's never the easy way," the witch muttered, crouching over my body. With unexplainable strength she lifted me from the floor and tossed me on the metal examining table, using leather straps to bind my legs, arms, and head.

Paralyzed, I more sensed than saw her do the same to Victor, but when she came back I stopped caring about Victor all together. Linva, that was her name—crazy the things you remember when you're trapped helplessly beneath an ice cream scoop—positioned her head so that her one toothed grin breathed hot on my face. "Time to wake up, Detective."

All I could manage was a gargled scream as the tool began digging into my eye.

Chapter 22

I woke up screaming, my face pulsing in rampant agony; flashes of haphazard surgery, rusty scissors and needles, haunting me as I sat bolt upright on the examining table. I grabbed my head with both hands as the worst migraine in existence made my skull its den. I hissed in pain, rocking back and forth, shouting obscenities until my throat burned. It was only when the pain changed from a jackhammer to a vice that I managed to pull my bloody hands away from my head. *Blood*, I thought, *I could see blood*. Hurriedly, I felt for my eyes, the excitement of finding them intact dulling the pain enough for me to hear the other sounds in the room.

It was as if a gong was going off every five seconds, metal ringing down the staircase with no concern for my condition. I heard vomiting to my right and turned to see Victor hunched over the other medical table, grasping at his head.

"You should leave now," a high pitched voice said from behind. I whirled in panic at the unfamiliar voice, a wash of colors clouding my consciousness as I did. Behind me stood a young girl, her face pale white and smooth beneath the red tint of the room. She had large eyes and two pigtails that fell to naked shoulders. Her smile was soft, her teeth showing just enough to make it genuine. She was gorgeous, her loin cloth and prehistoric bikini top reminding me of an Amazon flick I'd seen when I was a teenager.

I coughed to clear my throat. "Who—"

"They will take this place soon," the girl said. "There is another way out. Follow me."

Dazed by the metallic ringing, I watched as the girl moved deeper into the shadows toward the refrigeration units, blood dripping from her hands as she walked. "Move it, Detective!"

The inflection she used on the word 'detective' sounded familiar. "Linva?" I muttered, sliding to the floor. "I don't understand."

"You will,' she said. Pushing aside one of the corpses, Linva opened a unit on the bottom right where just enough light shone into the gap to reveal a small square air duct. "Help Victor please. I think he's in shock."

I stumbled over to Victor who was still gagging and grasping at his face. When I grabbed his arm his head snapped up. I recoiled in horror, crashing against the back side of the table.

"Look what she did!" Victor cried. "She changed me! She changed you…" Instead of looking at an eyeless gaze, I could see Victor's swollen eye sockets leaking tears of blood, just like Naomi had when they'd first arrived.

"Oh, get over it," Linva said impatiently, pacing the passage way. "Just grab him. We don't—"

There was a loud crash at the top of the staircase, and a strange violent buzzing noise began hurdling down towards us.

"That's not very nice," Linva said offended. "They brought explosives."

I yanked Victor to his feet, half dragging him to the small hole in the wall. "Push him through, push him through!" Linva said impatiently.

Victor suddenly snapped to, wrestling me off and running back to the medical table. "Where is it!?" He shouted wildly.

"Move it, Herse!" Linva shouted back.

"Got it!" Victor shouted excitedly as he threw his backpack over his shoulder.

I pull him back toward the air duct as he slipped on the last strap, but he ducked down into the passage voluntarily. Apparently I didn't follow fast enough.

"Good luck, Detective. " Linva said, shoving me ruthlessly after Victor.

I turned to see her smiling softly. The buzzing noise had become so loud that I barely heard her shouting. "The door is in the place you began! And Jared, don't you dare worry about me, worry about yourself. When you find you're stuck in a nightmare, always look for the lie!"

I opened my mouth to protest, but she slammed the door.

The explosion that followed a second later slammed my teeth shut, throwing me backwards. Darkness enveloped everything as metal twisted and churned beneath my hands and feet, and for the next thirty seconds it was like I was on a mad scientist's version of a space mountain.

"Linva!" I shouted, reaching back toward the opening as I stopped. "Son of a—!" I hissed as my hand shot back instinctively from the hot metal.

Victor groaned from behind. "Quiet down, Reign. She was just a witch."

"Did you see her?" I panted.

Victor laughed in pain. "Uhg-aaaly. Yeah, I saw her. Besides, the whore cut out our eyes! She got what she deserved."

"Karma?" I muttered.

I could hear Victor rest against the metal siding. "I don't believe in that crap," Victor muttered tiredly. "What did she do, Jared? If I had known this was what she had planned…"

Linva was the second person to tell me to not worry about them after dying for me. Why did people ever say that? It didn't help. Even if the last thing I'd seen was that old nasty woman… Some part of me felt that despite Linva's madness, she was far more important than we knew.

I sat back, closing my eyes. "Seriously, Herse, did you see her after you woke up? She was young. It's like she wasn't the same person. Whatever she did for us, at least the Loral and friends party don't seem to appreciate it."

"I'm surprised we can see at all." Victor sighed. "I guess knowing the enemy doesn't like her has to be good enough for now. Come on, let's move."

The air duct was cramped, making it difficult to move and breath, but the worst part was how long we crawled. At some point we'd fallen into water, at another we had to skirt a rat's nest, but it did give me time to think. My thoughts were foggy beneath my migraine, but I finally felt like we'd achieved something. I was moving forward, I thought, or maybe backwards as Linva had suggested, but either way I had more pieces to the puzzle of my family's murder. I was stumbling through this tower with a blindfold on, letting other people show me the way, and that felt dangerous. Within the cruelty and madness I was immersed in I barely recognized who I was. Seeing the video of Kelesa and Kara had reminded me of the outside world, what my life used to be like. I thought I was a bad person then, what was I now? The scary part was that the question didn't feel that important; what felt important was how all the people in the video loved Saints tower, how it was their modern miracle, and everything they ignored because of that. I still didn't know what this tower was, but the idea of loving any part of this place was repulsive.

The witch had wanted me to see something, to understand what Kelesa had done the days surrounding her death, but before I had time to think about it I bumped into Victor. It felt as if we'd crawled for an hour on bruised knees, but finally light had appeared ahead of us.

"Linva said that the door was where we began." I said quietly. "I assume that means Central Park."

We crawled the next hundred feet in silence until we were beneath a metal grate. "There's something wrong," Victor said as he looked up.

"What?"

"The sky is grey."

"What does that matter?" I asked impatiently, wanting to get out of this cramped space as soon as possible.

Victor didn't say anything as he pushed open the grate and crawled out. I followed him, but I stopped half way out and immediately understood what he meant. It wasn't the normal grey of storm clouds or of dusk, the sky was grainy with black specs moving like insects across its surface. Stranger still was the sun. It was beginning its decent toward the west, but it was solid crimson with no heat waves or light rays, leaving everything dull and washed out.

"Look," Victor said pointing. I followed his gaze towards the city where crows circled cracked and decayed buildings, and sidewalks and street signs where twisted and broken loose. Ash seemed to stream off of rooftops like waterfalls, billowing into clouds as they hit the bottom. Trees looked diseased and spotted, their branches reaching for the ground instead of the sky.

"Where are we?" Victor asked stunned.

It took me a few moments, but I knew exactly where we were. Kneeling in the middle of the wide street, hundreds of white clothed people stared at the buildings around them in reverent awe, taking in the abhorrent art show. I felt my stomach clench as my eyes traced each letter of the three different names spelled out in sprays of dripping blood. The grate had opened up on the edge of Times Square, and now I could see what Linva had shown Naomi.

Chapter 23

Ducking down behind a trash bin, Victor and I watched as a young man from the crowd held up his notepad, and the Master of Mirrors rang his bell. Through his dark sunglasses the Master of Mirrors gazed upon the name brought before him in elation, and for the first time I saw why he never touched the piece of paper. Black sludge oozed from each of his hands, dripping to the ground like steaming tar. His arms were solid black, and when he began etching the name upon his skin I knew why. What I thought had been a strange pen was really a tattoo gun, fueled by the hot ink of the man's own hands. Carved upon his flesh sat thousands of overlapping names, so many that only the new name was visible on his flesh.

As the Master of Mirrors raised his arm to the glass it began to liquefy, reaching out to his arm hungrily until it was devoured. When his arm was freed the new name was just another black splotch on the Master of Mirrors arm and mirror had adopted the ink.

"What is going on here," Victor whispered. "Why are the names written on the buildings? What kind of ritualistic crap is this?"

"I was hoping you would know that," I whispered back, making sure that no one was sneaking up behind us. "Catherine said something about the sandstorm putting them there."

"You spoke to Catherine?" Victor said shocked. "What else didn't you tell me?"

"Well, I definitely saw it different last time."

"So that's what the witch was doing…." Victor mused. "That's why that girl was screaming when we first got here. Turn around, Jared." As I turned, Victor looked me straight in the eye examining me. "You have green eyes now, like the ones I took—I can see them. She must have changed the way we see things." Victor took a moment to take in his surroundings again. "Everything we saw was a lie…everything they see is a lie."

I could see the eyes of the others now, but it was like a haze hung in front of them.

"That would explain why we couldn't see the door," I said.

"Forget the door," Victor said. "We need to break those mirrors."

"I agree," I said. "But we aren't getting anywhere close to them looking like this?"

Victor opened his backpack and pulled out a hand gun—my handgun. "Where'd you get that?!" I said, failing to muffle my voice.

"I pocketed it in the subway station—been a pain to keep hidden." He started to hand the Glock over to me, but hesitated. "I'm a lousy shot, but you…What really happened that night you killed all those people? I saw it on the news, but I've been meaning to ask you about that."

I ripped the gun away from him and checked the clip; there were four shots left. "I didn't miss if that's what you're asking."

"So the news was right," Victor said. "Good for you."

I glared at Victor for a moment before scanning the crowd again. "I need you to go find Catherine and bring her here. Once she's clear I'll take out the mirror. Then we use the chaos to head for the door."

Victor looked like he was about to protest, but scanned the crowd. "Where is she?"

I shrugged. "I'm not even sure what day it is. Last time she was near the edge on the west side."

"I'd hate to break this to you, but I don't see her."

My new eyes didn't see her either. I promised I would come back for her if we had a way out, but searching the city at leisure was impossible.

"Plus we have other problems," Victor said tightly.

I was about to ask what, when a darkness began crawling across the street, slowly covering the scribes in a blanket of shadow. Not too far in the distance, a towering cloud of browns and blacks was approaching the city like a tidal wave.

"Sandstorm," Victor groaned.

The Master of Mirrors raised his arms to the sky in admiration for the incoming storm, and then suddenly froze in confusion. He stared at the cloud for a few more seconds and then nodded, removing his sunglasses as he dropped his hands.

His eyes were pure white as he turned to stare right where I was hiding; they seemed to roll on water inside his skull. "We have forsaken amongst us," he said pointing in our direction. "The new messages must wait."

The scribes all pivoted their bodies so that they were looking in our direction, their white outfits rustling in the sudden wind. The street was darker now, the sand cloud casting half the sky into darkness, but I found Catherine. Tucked deep within the crowd, Catherine had her hand raised against her mouth, hiding her shock.

I gripped the Glock firmly. "Victor, Catherine is in the middle."

Victor shouted against the rising wind. "You've got to be kidding me. They are probably going to eat us in the next five seconds."

There was no time, so I stepped out from behind cover. "Catherine! I need you to come over here, right now."

"Well, that's much better," Victor grumbled sarcastically.

The crowd began to stand, but I lifted the Glock and pointed at the mirrors. "Keep em back, white eyes, or I'll shoot."

The man by the mirrors mouth tightened and I felt my muscles relax slightly, for all I knew those mirrors were indestructible.

"Don't move," he said in a deep commanding voice. The scribes obeyed, settling back into sitting positions. They looked frightened and confused, but not as frightened as Catherine. "Right now, Catherine," I urged. "This is your only chance. Make the choice. Us or the Tower."

I felt my palms grow sweaty as I kept my sight on the mirrors, waiting for any sign that my tenuous delay was going to be interrupted. As Catherine stared back at me, the light began fading quickly, the sandstorm leaving only a small break on the horizon, its howling wind changing into a disturbing buzz.

"Um, Reign," Victor said hurriedly. "She's not coming, and we need to get out of here."

"Give it a second," I said as I readjusted my aim.

"Jared, that sand is not sand!" Victor shouted.

I was going to turn to see what he meant, but Catherine finally stood, shaking from head to toe as she stepped around the crowd.

"Stop!" the man by the mirrors said. "This is not your fate." Catherine only froze for a second at the man's warning, but then picked up speed.

My eyes flickered toward the horizon; only a crack of light was left. I gave Catherine five more seconds to free herself from the crowd. "Grab her Victor," I shouted.

Victor moved quickly, running to Catherine and hauling her back towards us. I saw the Master of Mirror's eye sockets open wide as my finger tightened on the trigger. "Everyone stand!" He shouted wildly stepping in front of the mirrors. "Defend the mirrors with your lives."

I popped off two shots just as the light on the horizon winked out, casting the world into a haze of brown hues and tints. Then I shot a third. The sand hit me like an exploding avalanche, tossing me in the air and sliding me across the sidewalk threw a glass window. I twisted onto my stomach in time to see a wave of gnats' stream passed the window. A moment later Victor and Catherine hurdled through the broken window, landing hard next to me.

"Did you hit them?" Victor shouted desperately.

"He hit them," Catherine said sorrowfully. "The mirrors are broken—the voices are angry." Catherine began clawing at her head, her nails cutting lines into her skin. "So angry!"

I reached over and grabbed at her wrists. "You need to ignore them," I shouted. "Just follow me and Victor. We know the way out."

The gnats continued to swarm in massive balls outside, blinding me to anything on the other side. "This is our best chance," I shouted to Victor. "We can't see, but neither can they. We stood in the sandstorm when we first arrived, I don't think the bugs will do anything to us."

"They just threw you into a building!" Victor argued.

"Look, they've slowed down!"

Catherine wiped at her eyes. "What bugs?"

I stood, pulling Catherine to her feet. "That's what the sand is apparently. We can see things you can't. You'll just have to trust us."

"They said you tortured those women—"

I cut her off. "Trust us."

"Back here," Victor shouted. "This door leads to an alley way, it's not as bad here." I followed Victor's voice to where he stood holding open a door and peering out. "Ready?" he asked.

I nodded.

Stepping back into the storm felt like drowning in dirty rain. The gnats were everywhere, moving in strange patterns on top of us and around us. Moving felt like I was walking with my eyes closed, occasionally peeking between the spaces between my fingers to see what was ahead. Amid the wind and the gnats I was force to hold my hand against my nose, protecting it from invasion as I breathed. I could hear no others sounds other than the thunder booming above us, and the buzz swimming around us; if the scribes were close I couldn't tell. For a moment it felt as if we walked underneath a waterfall of disease as thousands of gnats started committing suicide against the sides of the buildings, exploding into thousands of tiny splashes of red, their tiny corpses raining down on us as we escaped.

"You see that!" I shouted to Victor. "The bugs leave the names behind."

"That pretty messed up, Jared, but that doesn't really help us."

By the time we put Times Square behind us the black and brown storm clouds on the east horizon began giving way to the eerie grey and black speckled sky. Then somewhere from within the chaos of gnats, ravaging wind, and shadows a hand grabbed my ankle. I looked down to see the white eyes of Master of Mirrors staring at me.

"You've accomplished nothing," he choked as he coughed up blood. "The Boss will always find a way. He won't abandon his people anymore. He promised. He'll still… send the names." The man went limp, and I could see the large hole where my third bullet had exited his back.

"Detective!" Catherine shouted. "Your leg is smoking!"

The black sludge from the man's hand had begun crawling up my leg, melting away my pants. Startled,

I was about to yank them off, but a swarm of locust redirected their flight toward me and encircled my leg. When they flew off my bare leg was clean.

"The sandstorm cleanses the city," Catherine said amazed.

Worried that Catherine would see that as some kind of Saints Tower miracle, I grabbed her hand. "Come on."

"Well ain't that great," Victor mumbled. "We just wasted our luck on your pants."

Chapter 24

The crimson sun haunted the corrupt sky again when Central Park came into view, the storms passing drawing the rotten city's residents back out into the open. We hid for as long as we could, but all it took was one hazy expression to send out the hounds. Hiding wasn't an option anymore.

Central Park forest felt sinister as we ran beneath the sagging trees, their twisted branches reaching out to slow our escape. The grass broke beneath our feet, dead from the elements, kicking up dust in our wake.

"She's coming," Catherine shouted.

I looked back at Catherine, seeing that our pursuers were only a hundred feet away. "Who?"

"Loral. She is very angry."

"Good," Victor said as he led us beneath a wooden bridge. "Means we are doing something right."

"Wait!" I shouted pulling Victor to a stop. "They'll be waiting for us out there."

Stepping in front of Victor, I peered out from the other side of the bridge. The small market set up on the other side was packed, but so far their attack programming hadn't been turned on. Like before they were relaxing and playing merrily, and eating…raw meat. I felt my skin turn to ice as I watched the vendors reach behind them into bags and hand out the hearts, livers, and kidneys as if they were candy—no…like they were apples. I felt my stomach get ready to rid itself of the sicking weakness consuming me, and I remembered Linva's comment about practice. This was in fact worst then the morgue.

I looked away, the image of people biting into fresh hearts sticking with me. "I think only those on duty are after us," I croaked weakly.

Victor pushed passed me, taking that as an all clear. "Their mistake."

I moved after him, but I wasn't surprised when he stumbled to a stopped upon seeing the decrepit sight. "I think I ate one of those,' Victor said, his face turning white. "I…I ate…"

I was so overjoyed at my minds avid shout that I hadn't eaten since arriving that I missed Catherine moving towards the vendor. She already had a heart in her hand, its red blood dripping down her hand as she went for a bite.

"Catherine!" My shout broke the reverie, but it gave me enough time to slap the apple out of her hand and pull her away from the crowd. One the girls that had slept with me the first night here was the first to point toward me. She was different than the others around her. Her skin was the color of ash, contrasting with the raven black hair whipped around her shoulders. Her lips were stained red from the feast, and while it might have just been my imagination expecting something wicked, when she shouted my name in excitement I thought I saw a forked tongue. Unfortunately that meant Victor had been right about something being wrong with them. Serial killers shouldn't be right…

I felt my body shiver in disgust as we pushed our way through the crowd and out of the cannibal market. I looked back long enough to see that the mob chasing us had halted for a second, sniffing at the air and turning back toward the hearts.

"I thought I felt a bit high after I ate that... ugh," Victor said disgusted. "Never thought addiction would be our salvation."

We slipped across the dead field, but as we drew closer to the place where we'd arrived yesterday the grass seemed to come alive. It was like we'd stepped into a peace summit between a hive of hairy spiders and a nest of diseased rats. They arrived in lines, crawled from the ground and across the street, scratching their way up the barren trees. We ran over the vermin, crushing the spiders and kicking the rats, but after a minute the park was covered in a wave of grotesque movement.

"That's amazing," Catherine said delighted as we came to a sudden stop. "It's an enchanted forest. Look at all the bunnies and butterflies."

"Bunnies and butterflies?" Victor said horrified as he kicked the rats off his legs. "Since when do butterflies crawl?"

Catherine's mouth twisted in confusion. "That is strange."

"I think I see the door," I said, breathing hard as I slapped at the spiders on my shoulders.

Victor looked at me with venom in his eyes. "Out with it."

"Over there," I said. "Look down." Amidst the army of nasty, there was one open spot visible on the ground. "Linva said we had to go down before we go up. That's gotta be what she meant. Look how they avoid it."

Victor nodded and then tried to move forward, but I held him back as I saw the rats and spiders begin to change directions towards us. "I doubt we'll make it that far."

"Then what do you suggest," Victor said desperately. "I don't know about you, but I hate rats."

I jumped as a scream behind us lodged my stomach in my throat. An older woman had just stepped away from the market, a half eaten organ in her right hand. In the time it took for me to realize what was happening, the rats had dragged the woman to the ground, prizing the spiders with a feast.

"What just happened!?" Catherine panted as the woman's screams died with her.

"See what you made me do!?" Loral screamed as she stepped across the field. As she walked, the rats and spiders moved to clear a path for her until she'd positioned herself in front of the door. Her gown of white was untarnished, as was her long braid of hair, but that was all that was still beautiful about her. Her face was the color of ash, webbed with blue veins, and when I saw her lidless white eyes I instinctively raised my Glock. I'd seen glittering specks of red on her skin before, but now I saw the source; small cracks of blood opened across her body, feeding the rats as they took turns tasting it, using her body to feed.

"If one rat so much as looks at me," I warned, "You'll die."

"You vile...I knew you'd be trouble, Jared Reign," Loral spat, "but I gave you a chance to live in my utopia, I took mercy on *you*."

The vermin's emotions seemed connected to Loral's as she started to snarl, hisses and chattering teeth increasing in volume. "And you Victor Herse, I gave you everything. Wasn't our night together passionate enough for you? Weren't the girls you requested for your twisted hobbies satisfying?"

Rats squealed and spiders jumped as they rippled with hatred at our feet. My fear was winning; I could feel it everywhere, deep in my bones, crawling on my skin. I didn't see a way out. All she had to do was sick her ocean of filth on us and it was over. But somewhere mixed in with the fear I managed to find just enough humor in the situation to have hope.

I looked at Victor with wide eyes. "Dang, Herse. You hit that?"

"Not cool, Reign," Victor said disgusted. "Beer goggles man, it's a rule, look it up."

The casualness of our banter sent Loral into a rage as she barreled towards us, ignoring the fact that I was holding a gun.

"What about me?" Catherine said suddenly.

The question caught Loral off guard and she stopped. "You're just a stupid girl," Loral said quickly. "Throwing away everything you could have ever wanted for these desecrators."

"You see how the rats react to the blood?" Victor whispered to me as Catherine began interrogating Loral. "I think they have a lust for it."

Catherine stood up tall, pointing behind her. "What about them? Are they stupid?"

Loral's face went slack as she took in the crowd trickling in behind us, the distraction of the feast apparently overcome.

"That old woman," Victor whispered. "I don't think Loral would have killed her on purpose. I don't think she can—"

"They are priceless," Loral sputtered in surprise. "Obviously."

"Did they see that you just killed one of them?" Catherine accused. "I think her name was Holly."

"Shut your mouth," Loral growled. "Beltin! End this. We shouldn't make a spectacle."

Victor's hand shot to his neck, pulling a small black dart from it. His eyes were wide as he looked at the dart, but I was already ducking behind Victor, pulling Catherine close. The next dart hit a few inches away from my head, imbedding itself in Victor's right thigh.

I only had time to see Beltin swing down from a tree before the rats and spiders converged on top of us. The sensation of spiders crawling all over my body created an instinctive flailing motion. Victor hit the ground, paralyzed from the darts, and Catherine screamed in terror as the rats began tangling in her hair.

Complete panic almost made me miss the fact that I wasn't being bitten or devoured. Summoning all of my willpower I ignored the coat of vermin covering my body and open my eyes. Somewhere between the spider legs and rat tails I was able to see Beltin walking toward us with a shotgun. It seemed Loral didn't want her followers to see a hoard of bunnies and butterflies eat three people alive.

Beltin was a normal looking guy, short brown hair, an athletic build, nothing creepy about him at all. I almost felt guilty at the look of surprise on his face when I shot him in the chest.

Like Victor had been trying to tell me earlier, it didn't take long for the rats thirst for blood to kick in. In less than five seconds the vermin had redirected to Beltin's bleeding body, swarming it like tiny land piranhas.

I had only a second to shake Catherine from her shock as Loral's shrill howl deafened me. I pointed at Victor who still laid flat on the ground, and then ran at Loral. I must have caught her by surprise as I tackled her to the ground, because she didn't start fighting back until I'd twisted her into a headlock.

Loral's fingernails dug into my forearms as I dragged her back toward the door, the veins on her face pulsing as I choked her. I was determined to put her out of the picture. I'd said I'd take out the tower's minions, and I meant it. As I fought with Loral's writhing, Catherine was busy dragging Victor's body, following as fast as her small frame would let her.

I stepped on the door, but the rats and spiders had finished their work on Beltin, turning back toward their mistress, and just as Loral's body went limp, I felt the first sharp stab on my leg. I ignored the bite and the five after that, dropping Loral and reaching down for the door handle. It was heavy, but when the white light shown through I felt invigorated despite the onslaught of venom and disease flowing through my body. I waited long enough for Catherine to drop Victor through the gap and jump after him, and then I rolled drunkenly through, taking dozens of Loral's pets with me.

Chapter 25

A faint drip of water echoed against cement walls as my eyes shot open. The orange electric lights flickering on and off like bug zappers above my head, sent cruel shivers of familiarity down my spine. My chest was rising and falling quickly, my breath frosty white in-between brief flashes of light. I sat up, my hands splashing up black water from beneath me. I tried to lie to myself, convince my own brain that it didn't know where I was, but this place... If it wasn't for the phantom pain of poison rushing through my veins I would have drown myself in the small puddle. *You're still in the tower*, I thought, clinging to the only thing that could be real. *If you weren't you'd be dead right now. Besides, you burned this place down. It doesn't exist.*

I stood slowly, the sounds of my movements crying like a howling wolf. I felt every muscle in my body cower in dread as I stared down the shadowy tunnel. The forgotten subway tunnel was narrow enough for two people, abandoned years ago near the docks of eastern Manhattan. I glanced around for Victor and Catherine, but I already knew I was on my own. I'd visited this place hundreds of times before in nightmares, and I was always alone.

I took a tentative step forward and stopped before I could take another. *I can't go back there*, I thought. *Not again.* Flashes of fire, screams, cages, and paparazzi tortured my nerve as I stood staring in the darkness. Saints Tower had appeared only a month before I'd turned in my badge...it hadn't helped then either.

I turned to walk the other way, but was met with a solid brick wall. *That's wrong*, I thought, sliding my fingers across its cool, rough surface. I felt a chill touch my skin and looked down at my shredded clothes. *So is that. I was in a suit last time I was here. There's your evidence, Jared. It's not the same place. It's just the tower playing tricks on your mind, toying with you. You're use to this.*

Slowly, I reached behind my back for my Glock. Thankfully it had made the trip, but when I checked the clip it was empty—its last bullet lodged in Beltin's chest. The feel of the metal in my hand, and knowing I'd beaten the tower again gave me the courage to turn around. I had to keep going. I had to be closer to figuring this out.

The faulty lighting gave the impression that the tunnel would go on forever, but a metal door appeared to my right after only a few strides. Years ago the officers with me had to break the door down, but this time I just turned the handle and it creaked open, a loose piece of metal grinding across the cement. *Stop thinking it's the same,* Jared. *This is different.*

Old scaffolding and planks rested against unpainted cement walls while fishing net, rope, and old cans of paint thinner took up most of the floor. The old storage room was mostly normal, but the cages and massive wooden shipping containers always reminded me of an abandoned animal shelter meant to survive a fallout.

My hands let go of the door and hooked themselves around my neck as I rocked back and forth on my feet, both terrified and relieved. It was the same room, but more importantly it was empty.

Neilson Ki and Reese Walters had been arrested on suspicion of extortion, prostitution, and murder, only to be released after the judge didn't find significant evidence to incarcerate them. I'd played it by the book, collected evidence, determined motive, and even got a confession to all but the murders. Needless to say, when they were put back on the streets I just about lost it. I followed them for days—sleeping in my car, living off of fast food and coffee, until they led me to here. It took two more weeks to get the warrant, but when I did, what I found was appalling. Most nights I could still see the men and women huddled in the cages, drinking water out of dog dishes, stripped naked with no blankets, waiting to be stuffed inside boxes to be shipped. And the others...the moans of the slow, dying, discarded remnants of a massive human trafficking cartel. Victor asked me why I killed those people, this room was why.

There was a tap on my shoulder. I flipped around, my nose meeting the grinning face of a red headed woman. She would have been beautiful if her face wasn't heavily scared and practically held together by fresh stitches. I recoiled back, using the cages to stay upright. Behind her, five similar women followed, each holding a single butchers knife in their right hand—a parade of adult horror dolls, each dressed in red high heels and short skirts.

I prepared myself for an attack, but the girls just smiled softly at me and walked past. *That's definitely different*, I thought frantically, my adrenaline short-circuiting my brain. Their shoes clicked against the hard wooden planks, moving toward the back of the room where a single florescent bulb hummed patiently.

Cautiously, and stupidly, I followed, my eyes searching the room for anything I could use as a weapon while I walked passed crates and cages; but unless I wanted to wield a can of paint thinner or a grimy mattress I was out of luck.

The muffled cries came suddenly, and I sank back, ducking behind the cargo container the girls stepped into. Tentatively I peeked inside.

Victor sat in a wooden chair that was bolted to the ground. Tied and gagged, sweat pouring off his face, he struggled violently to get free of the bolted down prison as the women stepped towards him, surrounding him on each side.

I turned at the sound of another muffled scream, and saw Catherine against the back wall choking on a white cloth as a silent heart-rate monitor spiked wildly on the screen next to her. Outfitted in a blue hospital gown that left her stomach exposed, Catherine hands shook beneath the restraints of the medical bed, but I could tell that the Multiple IV's running into each arm had weakened her fight.

Something or someone grabbed me from behind, pushing something sharp into my neck as I twisted. The world tilted as I was shoved aside, sending me crashing into another cage. I held onto the bars for support as I turned back to see two people in white doctors coats standing there. One was wiping a large needle clean with a white cloth. My head began pounding like thunder, and the light of the room suddenly became painful enough that a thousand of those needles seemed friendly.

The muffled screams amplified as the doctors moved towards Catherine, each producing a scalpel from their pockets. I only had time to watch the doctors begin cutting into her stomach before I felt the pain of fire touch my skin. I fell to the floor screaming as my arm burst into light, the sound of shattering glass cutting into my skin. Another bottle of glass shattered near my head, and I turned, squinting against the slow burning flames of twenty or so Molotov cocktails, screaming as I saw the faces of the people I had murdered five years ago.

Chapter 26

Nielsen Ki and Reese Walters jolted out of their conversation as we burst through the door, sending beer bottles crashing to the ground. It only took them a few seconds to grab the 9 mm and the illegal AK from the desk next to them. My eyes flickered to the sickly people around me, and back to the criminals as I targeted them. Coughing and crying moans of help distracted me as I tried to speak. "Drop the weapons!"

Nielsen Ki was first generation Asian American, his black hair and sharp eyes making him look fearless. He reached for his belt and grabbed what looked like a set of keys. "You let us out and I'll give you these. Otherwise…" Nielsen held the keys to his side, jingling them over a small sewage drain. "Your choice."

"This is sick," Officer Kevin Loury whispered. "These are probably the ones they couldn't sell or ship."

Officer Devon Lez's stony face looked dangerous. "Looks like quite the haul," he shouted. "If I had to guess there is probably a couple hundred grand piled up behind you, was it worth your soul? Give us the keys and tell us where the others went."

"Too late," Nielsen shouted, half crazed. "They left the country yesterday. Time's ticking boys." He made a tick tock noise as he fumbled with the keys.

I felt my heart shrivel up. How many more people had they taken since they'd been freed?

"Aright, alright," Kevin said lowering his weapon. "Let us get these people out, and we'll walk away."

"What you think Reese?" Neilson said, training his weapon on Kevin.

"I think we'll be out by Monday," Reese said, flicking open a Zippo lighter. "Can't convict someone without evidence."

"Or witnesses," Neilson said.

As Reese tossed the Zippo lighter, the AK burst to life, but I'd already pulled the trigger. I shot five more times, feeling my rage burst out with each shot. I couldn't believe how this could have happened. How many people should have been saved? Monsters like this shouldn't get the chance to be free. I saw Reese's and Neilson's bodies fall, but I kept shooting.

"Reign!" Devon shouted as my gun clicked empty. "Kevin's hit!"

I kept my eye trained on the two fallen bodies at the end of the room. "Get him out of here. I'll get the others out.

"You better hurry," Devon said. He pointed to the corner of the room where Reese's Zippo light had ignited the paint thinner. "This room's covered in dry wood. Probably their escape plan."

`I sprinted to the end of the room and crouched over Neilson's body; even in death he looked fearless. Quickly, I grabbed his hand and fumbled for the keys, but they were gone. I scrambled across the floor, running my hands against the wooden baseboards. I glanced over my shoulder to call for Devon, but he was already gone and the flames were already licking the ceiling and crawling across the scaffolding. Smoke became thick as I dove towards the sewer grate. The sensation of emptiness surrounding my hand as it searched the drain was horrifying. Without those keys these people were trapped.

I pulled my hand out and spun around, grabbing Reese's Assault rifle and running toward the cages. Fire exploded as the scaffolding began to collapse towards the floor. My eyes stung with smoke as I found the lock of one of the cages and tried to force it open with brute force. When that didn't work I took aim and fired. The cage opened, but my heart sank. The weakened people in the cage were already unconscious from breathing in the smoke. The fire was surrounding them causing their skin to steam as their sweat began to boil.

I got four of them out before the fire consumed the whole room. I'd saved four, and killed a dozen; all because I didn't want the bad guys to get away. They said I'd done the right thing, shot defensively to save Kevin's life, but I knew otherwise. I'd shot to kill. If I hadn't, maybe I would have found the keys—maybe all those people would still be alive.

Chapter 27

My eyes shot open as I inhaled wildly, the buzzing lights above me cheering at my agony. I screamed as soon as my lungs found their meal, my arms lashing out at nothing. I could still taste the fire, feel it burning through my skin and muscle. I could feel the horror of each nerve ending as they overloaded with suffering until they were dead.

I swung my head around frantically, desperate to wash away the memory of the pain, screaming Kelesa's name while the buzzing lights and distant drips of water warned me that I was still trapped.

My throat was hoarse by the time my body had calmed, forgetting the flames and basking in the puddle beneath my back. I sat up, trembling with the idea that I was still in the tunnel that lead to the *room*. Why did I go back in? I thought weakly. This was the second time I'd awoken after being cooked alive. The first time after being burned alive should have been enough. I'd tried to free Victor and Catherine, but it had all ended the same. *It's a loop*, I thought. *No not a loop. I should be dead, but they keep me alive after they burn me.* I could see the bright lights of the hospital room where they cared for me, healed my burns with herbs and medicine as I tried to say sorry. Then I woke up in the tunnel so they could do it all over again.

It took hours to collect my strength to stand up. I could practically sense the door calling for me to open it, begging me to suffer again. I took a few steps forward and then back, pacing, trying to shake away the fear leeching my thoughts. "What's the point in this!?" I shouted. My voice echoed down the tunnel, but there was never a response. Stubbornly I sat against the wall and closed my eyes. I fingered my Glock wishing it wasn't empty. *At some point I'll die from starvation*, I thought. *Unless they can heal that as well… How long is this going to happen to me?*

It started off as a soft icy wind, the lights on the ceiling swaying, but then I could hear the whispers. "We're waiting. We're waiting."

I cringed at the haunting sound, gripping my empty Glock as if it would protect me. "I'm not going back in there…" I stammered.

The wind changed to a violent blizzard, the puddle beneath my feet turning to ice. "You're friends are already here," the whispers hissed. "They are dying to see you."

"I know!" I shouted. "It doesn't matter!"

From the shadows of the tunnels the red headed women appeared, their butcher knives covered in frozen blood. They smiled at me, beckoning me to follow them as the first one spoke. "We can't begin without you. Please help us."

I stumbled away, slipping on the ice as I tried to stand. "Who...who are you?" I asked.

"We are bored," the girl in the back chimed childishly. "You're making us bored."

"We can do this the easy way or the…" I stopped to listen as a thought jumped into my mind, the phrase reminding me of Linva, the witch. *When you are trapped in a nightmare, search for the lie.*

Instantly my mind began analyzing everything it had seen—the girls, the captives, the doctors; they were strange, frightening even, but were they a lie? The room, maybe it was the room. I knew that room perfectly, but it had been exactly how I remembered it—no lies there. The hospital bed and Victor's chair were different, maybe...

The doctors stepped up behind the girls, white coats already bloodied, their hair covered in flakes of snow. "We can't sew her up until you come. With no drugs she'll go mad from the pain."

My hands shook enough that I dropped the empty Glock and had to scoop it back up. "I'm not going back in that room!"

"Coward," one of the girls pouted. "A little fire and he has already given up. At least Victor lets us play."

I didn't realize I was backing away until my back hit the wall. *The lie,* I thought excitedly as I turned to face the wall. I ran my hands across the rough surface of the brick, looking for anything that would help me.

"Oh no," one of the girls gasped.

"Drag him back," one of the doctors ordered surprised. "Drag him back now!"

My fingers fumbled desperately as I heard the group running toward me, finding nothing but mortar and brick. I kicked at the wall, I spat at it. I slammed the butt of the Glock into the middle, and then fell through, straight into rush hour traffic.

Chapter 28

Horns blared, cars swerved, taxi drivers cursed. I watched stupidly as a car forced a motorcycle onto the sidewalk to avoid hitting me while another squealed to a stop a few inches away from taking out my legs.

Coffee had spilt across the driver's windshield and dashboard, distorting the man's anger as he glared at me. "Get off the road you lunatic," he barked, opening the door. I stared at the man incredulously as he stepped out and grabbed a baseball bat—he was completely *normal*. "I said get out of my way!" the man shouted, smacking the bat into his palm.

I raised my hands in the air, surrendering. The man's eyes went wide as he dropped the baseball bat, and I turned, panicked that the horror dolls and doctors were still behind me. "Don't shoot," the man pleaded as he climbed back in his car. "I got family." I looked up to see my Glock glinting in the sunlight, and turned back to the man apologetically.

Finally my brain pistons began moving again. Holstering the gun quickly, I moved off the street and onto the sidewalk, annoying at least ten New Yorker's on the way. I found a bench covered with a law firm advertisement and sat down, probably looking like someone on drugs as my eyes darted around wildly.

A pleasant thought teased me as I tracked the hustle and bustle of New York. Maybe, just maybe I'd escaped the Tower. This place seemed normal enough, there wasn't anything trying to kill me yet. I grabbed my head between both hands, blocking out the world as I tried to think. I never found out why my family had been killed, but enough was enough, I wasn't sure I could take anymore.

A man sat down next to me opening a newspaper. I looked over to see a picture of Saints Tower on the front page, an announcement of the new names for the day. I felt my teeth grind instantly, feeling a sense of bitter resentment and loathing. Even if I was out of the tower, I didn't want to live with that thing still standing.

"Kelesa Reign," the man next to me said. "Isn't that the wife of that cop that got all those people burned alive?"

My mouthed dropped open and my body went ridged at the sound of my wife's name. The man was still looking down at the paper, and was just about to turn the page before I ripped it from his hands.

He held out his hands like he was still holding the paper. "Hey!"

My eyes flickered to the announcement on the page where it read: SAINTS TOWER HAS REVEALED TWO NEW NAMES TODAY. IT WAS A PLEASANT SURPRISE TO SEE KELESA AND KARA REIGN, WIFE AND DAUGHTER TO FORMER DETECTIVE REIGN, GIVEN SUCH SUPPORT FROM THE TOWER. MANY SAY IT'S JUST ANOTHER EXAMPLE OF HOW THE TOWER REPRESENTS EVERYONE. I felt my fists crumple the newspaper. The date at the top was the same day they had died.

"Hey," the man next to me said again. "At least give it back."

I tossed the man the crumpled paper in a daze, red fire blurring my vision. "How old is that newspaper?" I asked coolly.

"I bought it like thirty seconds ago," the man said annoyed, failing in his effort to smooth out the thin pages. "You need some help, buddy."

I felt my pulse in my stomach, beating quickly as I tried to catch my breath. I knew it was impossible, my family had died weeks ago, maybe even longer, but the idea tortured my mind. I tried to focus, tried to find out where my mind was. If I'd lost it, actually gone crazy like I'd thought back with the vipers, would I even know it. Maybe I was just one of them now. Or maybe this was just another part of the tower, a place that…

"Look," the man said next to me. "I think that's her."

I hesitated for a moment, just staring at the man's finger as he pointed to the corner of the street. In some deep hidden corner of my mind I expected what I saw, but it didn't prepare me for the guttural fear I felt. Wanting something so badly, so desperately that nothing else mattered, left me locked in the thought that if it wasn't real I would cease to exist. A few steps away, at the edge of the street, Kelesa flagged down a cab while Kara jammed to her headphones.

I was half way to them before I told my feet to move, my focus zeroed in like a starving hawk. My wife's soft smile felt like a warm fire, welcoming me in, her glossy red hair flaring out as she turned to face me. Kara freed one of her ears of music as she pulled a fancy cell phone out of her pocket, but fumbled as she looked up at me. Both Kelesa's and Kara expressions changed as they saw me walk toward them, twisting into confusion and surprise.

"Kelesa!" I called out, shoving passed a pedestrian.

"Yes?" she said, backing away. "Do I know you?"

The question was similar to being shot. At first I was confused. Then it dug in deep like a parasite, the pain spreading from beneath, twisting and biting. And then I felt a primal rage, a surge of adrenaline that sent me into survival mode, my brain warning me that I was on the verge of death. The tower had played my heartstrings, made me dance right into its trap. The slap of realization that it wasn't real was as sharp as any knife.

Kelesa's smirk was practically gushing with pity as she shook off her confusion and took a step toward me. "Is there something I can help you with? You look lost. Maybe I could buy you some new clothes."

Before I could respond a cab pulled up on the curb.

"Mom," Kara called. "Dad's on the phone."

My eyes flickered to Kara's phone as Kelesa opened the cab's door and ducked in. "What do you think?" she said to Kara as she kept one eye on me. "Do we tell him now or wait until dinner? Come on get in."

Her words washed over in me in a wave of déjà vu. I felt Kara's next words on my lips as she said. "He sounds busy."

As Kara handed Kelesa the phone I grabbed her arm, pulling her away from the cab.

"Hey!" Kelesa shouted, clambering out of the car. I pulled Kara against my chest, shielding her against injury. "Someone help! He's got my daughter!"

Kara's body went limp. I tried to readjust for the dead weight, but too late I realized that she had just used a defensive move I'd taught her when she first started to go out with her friends. She twisted as she fell, freeing herself as I slackened my grip. I tried to grab her again, but someone from behind me wrapped their arms around my neck, dragging me backwards. As I elbowed the person in the face, Kelesa grabbed Kara, pulling her into the cab, shouting at the driver to go.

"Kelesa!" I shouted wildly, fighting off more attackers. "Get out of the car! Please!"

The cab's tires squealed as it took off down the street. I turned to chase, barely noticing the three people with bloody noses as I tore after the cab, pleading desperately with the cab to stop. I knocked over a food cart as I spun around to an oncoming crowd, tripping into the streets. I stopped more traffic, but didn't care. That phone call...it was the last I'd ever heard from them. Right now, on the other end of the line, I was explaining how I'd gotten the girl, Pren, released, but Benjamin had called me in for some last second advice and I wouldn't be able to meet them for dinner.

The cab driver stopped at a red light. I felt a flood of hope rush through me as I closed the distance. I could see the back of Kelesa's head in the back as she handed the phone back to Kara.

It was as if Kara was whispering in my ear. "Tell Uncle Ben to let you get home early. We have a surprise for you. Love you dad."

Metal crunched as the back of the cab was struck from behind by a silver SUV, tires grinding against the asphalt until the cab was left in the middle of the intersection. A scary calm settled over me as I watched the waste management truck collide with the left side of the cab, flipping it like a child's toy into the other side of traffic where it spun into the front of another cab.

I didn't understand it. I felt all my feelings shut off; like a button was pressed that stopped the current of emotion. Why was I seeing this?

Cars piled up on both sides of me as I tried to get to Kelesa and Kara. Glass shattered, horns blared, air bags deployed; I could sense the chaos around me, I even felt the cars threaten to pin me against one another, but I just trudged through the carnage until I was looking into the shattered back window of the cab.

Kelesa was holding Kara in her arms. She could have simply been comforting her daughter after a long day. It was almost beautiful, but I had to look away when the red began running off her forehead.

I staggered away from the car drunkenly, feeling the dread begin poisoning my veins. I could barely breathe—the memory of losing them growing fresh in my heart. I'd been distracted, tossed into the tower's world without answers, but seeing my family's death happen first hand—powerless to stop it—was unbearable. I kept moving, stepping around the injured and putting any space I could between me and the source of the torment. There was no comfort anywhere, I was alone—lost and robbed of happiness. I begged my sorrow to channel into anger, but this time it lingered, seeping into every particle of my being. It was worse than any nightmare; it burned more than the fire of the room.

Somewhere buried within all the hurt I felt one thought slip through. I stumbled into a traffic light post, and looked up, tears blurring my vision. *Look for the lie*, my mind whimpered. *Make it make sense. You know that crash was no accident.*

My eyes scanned the scene, watched as the police and ambulances arrived. Most of the people seemed fine, a few bumps and bruises, probably only a few law suits. Most of the cars were going to need repairs though; smoke puffed from beneath hoods, cheap poly-carbon paneling was left cracked and bent. Amidst the small bubble of carnage, only one vehicle looked undisturbed. The silver SUV was reversing, struggling to find enough room on the one way street to make a U-turn.

My feet fell heavily on the asphalt as I began moving towards my family's killer, each step taking a herculean feat to accomplish. My pace quickened as I became more focused, but the SUV was on its last leg of its six point turn. Just as the car was about to escape through the crowd of traffic, I grasped the door handle and ripped it open, reaching in and dragging the driver out of his seat as the SUV jumped forward.

The man wailed as he was thrown to the ground, his bowler hat tumbling down the street as he hit the ground. He gasped as the air was knocked from his lungs, his hands rising defensively to shield his face. I wrestled with the man's arms, trapping them beneath my legs, twisted them until the man screamed, and then I looked into his frightened glassy eyes.

"Ben?"

It took me several moments to wrap my mind around seeing my best friend. "How? W—why?"

The baleful grin that suddenly took over Benjamin's face turned my blood to ice. It was almost inhuman, twisted to the point that twenty years of friendship couldn't make it identifiable.

"Opps," Ben said maniacally as he rolled beneath me. I let the motion happen and even watched as Benjamin shuffled back into the SUV and drove off. I should have been confused, drawn into a deep chasm of shock, or at the least vengeful, but all I felt was a slow feeling of understand. Pieces of the puzzle began falling into place; questions that had eluded me, that had subconsciously driven me insane, those questions that had tied me to an existence of mystery, they were all evaporating, freeing me of a debilitating denial.

Benjamin had called me into work, sent me on a fool's errand that he could have handled alone, all so he could get Kelesa and Kara alone. He'd loved the Tower, always jealous that his name hadn't appeared on the mirrors. Even after seeing it, I still found it hard that he could have killed my family, he loved Kelesa and Kara. But whether it was true or not, the revelation made me begin envisioning the street I was standing on differently. I could see the light around me dim as I remembered standing here a few days ago, afraid and desperate to stay silent. The cars faded, the frantic activity slowing to stillness where nothing except the shuffling footsteps of vipers rang in my ears. I knew this street. I'd walked down in a dozen times without ever realizing this was where my family had died. Clearly I was in the Tower, and if I was than there had to be a door—and I thought I knew where it was.

I walked carelessly down the street and around the corner, ignoring everyone's worried questions as I pushed through the crowd of onlookers that had appeared. My target was tucked away between a tax relief business and a dry cleaners, but Cloud Nine pawn shop stood open for business.

A small bell jingled as I pushed open the glass door, the smell of coffee waffling up from the back. The odds and ends of collecting for years lined and hung from walls, small yellow price tags hanging from each item. I stepped up to the counter and looked down over the weapons inside the glass counter. I was just about to reach over and ring the bell on the counter as a young woman with raven black hair and a rosy smile greeted me. Her gentle eyes seemed to sparkle as she looked over me empathetically. I knew her, but she looked different surrounded by ordinary life.

"You made it," Linva said softly. "By all that is miraculous and sexy, you made it." I started to open my mouth, but Linva held up a hand and cut me off. "You may think you know the truth detective, but there is still one more step you must take. Follow me, and I'll show you to the door. That is why you're here isn't it?"

I nodded and followed her into the back room. "I could use some of the weapons," I said as the door came into view.

I'd seen the double mirrored doors many times, but this time they were set into an elegant white wall that was decorated with hieroglyphic, just like they had been outside. The symbols glowed golden, pulsing in and out of sight with each breath.

"I'd love for you to take weapons to the top of the tower," Linva said with an evil little laugh. "Oh if I could only see his face…" she sighed. "But the door won't let you."

"What am I supposed to do?" I asked as she opened the door.

"Don't ask me," Linva said shrugging. "You're the one that wanted to climb the tower. I'd suggest making the trip worth it. Come on, up you go."

"Any hints?" I said shaking my head. "What about Victor and Catherine?"

Linva's frown almost made her look like a small child that had just lost her doll. "Oh they'll be waiting for you, although they didn't handle things as well as you, the door they found…we'll let's just say I wasn't there." Linva smiled again as she motioned me forward. "I don't have all day."

She shoved me as I got closer to the doors white light, but I resisted, and took a step back. "I don't think I have anything left in me, Linva. I know who killed my family, but it just feels empty."

She smiled softly. "Then you're right where we all need to be, Jared. The most important question of all is why. You know who, but do you know why? All answers can be found at the foot of a child's bed, we just have to be willing to bend down and take a look."

"What the Sam hell does that mean—" I said. Her shove was harder this time, but I didn't resist, letting Saint Tower have its way with me, hoping this time I wouldn't wake up.

"Make sure you give my best to the *Boss*," Linva's voice said, following me into the white void.

Chapter 29

Feathers lazily floated in the air; dropping so slowly they seemed frozen in time. I'd fallen fiercely onto a white bed when I'd arrived, its wooden frame cracking in two near my feet as I landed, dropping half the mattress to the floor. My head rested comfortably on a pillow as dusty grey light shown down on me from where I'd broken through the ceiling. Light from beneath a lamp shade to my right failed to show anything but the side table it stood on, but the wooden paneled blinds, tucked behind shadowy curtains, hinted at a storm outside.

It felt surprisingly calm in the silence of the dark room, like snuggling up in blankets when the power went out during a blizzard. I felt hollowed out from my last few experiences in the tower, and it took me several minutes to decide to move. I was afraid, fragile to the point of shattering. I'd never felt like that before, vulnerable and weak, but why be strong?

When I tried to move my arms I couldn't, but that was fine. The black straight jacket gave me a sense of security; protecting me from lashing out in a frustration I undoubtedly couldn't control anymore. I'd been in the tower for too long, seen too many twisted things, and felt too much hate. The tower had given me the illusion that I was in control of what was happening, but now the delirium had gone and I didn't know if I trusted myself.

I rolled out of the bed, my bare feet kicking up dust as they hit the hardwood floor. I felt hard metal pressing against my skin where my jeans started on my back. For a moment I struggled to grab my Glock, but I knew I wasn't Houdini and gave up quickly, turning my attention to the door. A small metal window in the door slid open and a pair of eyes peered in curiously. When the woman saw me it was like she'd seen a dragon.

"Hi," I said.

Gasping, she stepped back far enough that I could tell that she had short spiky hair. "The Doc warned us about you," she said. "He told us to not speak with the ones that fall from the sky."

I stood still, trying to look as passive I could. "Maybe that's because he doesn't want you to know something." I said conspiratorially.

"Like what?" the woman said confused.

"That's enough, Cindy." The girl's eyes disappeared from the hole and the door opened. A bald man with chocolate brown skin, dressed in a black medical coat stepped into the room. He was my height with deep wrinkles on his forehead, and he seemed tired. "Hello, Mr. Reign. I am Doctor Dane. May I ask you some questions?"

Ignoring the man, I peered beyond him into a long metallic hallway lined with doors. "Where am I?"

"You are in a psychiatric ward, Mr. Reign. It is my job to help those who are not prepared for what they will find outside."

My eyes traveled to the spiky haired girl. She also wore a straight jacket, and was now running to each door, kicking or head-butting them, signaling the room's occupants to come see the newcomer. It didn't take long for most of the hallway to become filled with onlookers.

"See, there's a forsaken here," Cindy said. "I told you." The idea set off an instinct to huddle together, and they stared at me as if I was there to steal their first born child—only I didn't see any children.

"Forsaken?" I muttered under my breath.

"Yes, forsaken," the doctor said. "It means abandoned."

"Abandoned by what?" I asked, eyeing the clipboard in his hand.

He thumbed through the pages robotically and looked up at me. "Abandoned by destiny, fate, karma, whatever you want to call the forces that move the universe. You have been left in nakedness, fueled by your own passions and nothing else. You are dangerous."

"That doesn't sound so bad."

The crowd of people rippled with discomfort as the doctor jotted down a few notes. "I'd love to understand you a bit more. I feel you have many issues we could address. I would like to start with why you killed so many people. There are about a dozen people here that would like to know the same thing.

"Huh?" I said puzzled.

"When people die in the tower, they don't just die, Mr. Reign. They come here, unprepared and usually unstable. You have sent many people to me. I want to know what drove you to that action."

"Survival," I said coldly.

"Interesting," the Doctor said. "It's a shame really. Usually I'd keep you here under evaluation until you were prepared to face the truth, but He told me send any forsaken straight to see him. Please follow me."

The psychiatric ward was huge, and it took several minutes to walk through to the security station at the other end. The Doctor buzzed us through a gate and then led me outside.

Heavy clouds of gold, white, and black hung like frozen sentinels over a lush field of green grasses and shadowed flowers. There was no wind, no sound, but the taste of a fresh rainstorm was in the air. Black winged creatures darted across the sky, and in the distance a waterfall of ice dropped from a cliff, impossibly emptying itself into a lake of brimstone and fire. I knew I was somewhere high because the ground I stood on ended about a hundred yards away, giving way to wisps of cloud cover that surrounded the occasional rooftop of a skyscraper.

"Watch your step," the doctor said. "He lives over there."

In front of me—across a thin stone, arched bridge—stood an enormous white mansion. Statues of bronze angels guarded the bottom of two large staircases leading up to a roman-styled water fountain. Black roses lined the edges of dozens of glaring windows, and behind it stood the white spear of the tip of Saints Tower.

I stepped onto the bridge and looked down, vertigo hitting me fast and hard as I saw the New York skyline spread out beneath me. I took a moment to take in the sight, feeling that it was likely the last beautiful thing I'd ever see, and then I moved towards the mansion.

The doors were wide open, carrying out the sweet and sour smell of sweat and sex. I stepped into a royal greeting hall, a narrow room that stretched deep into the core of the mansion. King size beds lined the walls on either side, doorways branching off into other parts of the mansion tucked between them. Bodies writhed in pleasure beneath white linen sheets as I moved through the enormous hallway, each bed a different scene of bodily pleasure. At the end, surrounded by a crowd of ball-gowns and tuxes, Victor and Catherine stood out in their black straight-jackets.

Next to them, Loral looked dazzling in her long pink, silky skirt, split so that one of her endless legs revealed itself wantonly, her sparkling corset leaving little to the imagination. I would have berated myself for my pavlovian response, but the man in the middle blinded me to everything else.

Benjamin Hart, my best friend and business partner, glared straight at me as I moved closer. I could see astonishment in his eyes, but he merely adjusted his bowler hat and waited. As I walked onto the dance floor I could see that Victor and Catherine were not normal, their dispositions reminding me of vipers.

"Someone explain this to me," Benjamin said regally, sharp lines appearing on his jaw. "How is *he*, here?"

"He's the one that killed sister, Daddy," Loral said sadly. "He's the one that's been traveling with these two." Loral patted Catherine and Victor on the face sharply.

"I know that," Benjamin said annoyed. "How did he get here? I really do hate party crashers, Mr. Reign."

Chapter 30

There are moments that open your mind to the intangible, times when you're forced to see beyond what makes sense and what is real—I hate those times. I stared at my ex-best friend. That's what I did, but I knew that wasn't what I was doing. "You're not Ben," I said flatly.

He chuckled. "No, I am not. But you have invaded my tower, killed one of my daughters, so forgive me if wearing the face of the man that killed your family bothers you."

I failed to hide the venom as I spat, "Who are you? Why did you kill my family?"

"Pay attention Detective. Like I said, that *was* Benjamin. I merely nudged him in the right direction. Mammon is like playing with puppet strings."

"You didn't answer my questions," I said.

"So bold," Loral said dreamingly. "You sure I can't have him? Beltin was a wonderful pet, but this one would be absolutely sinful." Loral fingered the bruises on her neck gingerly. "Plus, I like it rough."

Benjamin walked over and took a wine cup from one of the crowd, brushing Loral's arm affectionately as he passed. "You don't deserve to hear my name, Detective, but your family is dead for a very simple reason. They rejected me."

"You mean they rejected the tower."

Benjamin shrugged. "It's all apples and oranges. How about we find some privacy? I'd hate to ruin everyone's fun. Victor, Catherine, feel free to join us. I've showed you off enough for one day."

Victor and Catherine barely glanced my way as they zombie walked after Ben. I could sense something different about them, like an unsettling pain that couldn't be expressed. I moved after them slowly, trying to put together any pieces of the puzzle I could before I was blindsided again, but I had nothing to work with.

Eventually we stepped into an elevator and Benjamin pushed a button marked ground floor. Benjamin sipped at his wine, letting each droplet linger on his tongue before tasting the next. I tried to catch Victor's attention, but it was like he was staring into oblivion.

Ben tapped his fingers against the wine glass. "Do tell me, Mr. Reign. How did you end up here? I was waiting for you at the door, but you never showed up with your friends. I fidgeted nervously as the elevator continued dropping; the part of my brain that fired off warning signals had been overloaded after seeing Kelesa and Kara die, but something felt very wrong.

"Why do you get to have all the secrets?" I said.

The elevator dinged, opening its doors upon an oddly tinted garden. It was beautiful, the hues of grey and black making the reds and greens pop like red lipstick in a black and white movie. Horses snorted as they pulled carriages down stunning streets, the wheels of the carts rolling over dark green grasses, trimmed short like a golf course. Further in the distance people laughed over a newspaper article while drinking tea and coffee, and despite being surrounded by flowers on every side, Mother Nature couldn't hide the fact that I was in the center of a bustling city.

I followed Benjamin out of the elevator for several steps and watched the door slide shut, leaving nothing behind but the smooth white surface of Saints Tower.

Benjamin produced a cigar from the inside of his jacket and cut off the end. "I do love secret passages, don't you? But I suppose that doesn't help me at the moment. Perhaps I could change your mind if I share a few of my secrets?"

"Sure," I said distractedly. Victor and Catherine had moved automatically to a patch of grass beneath a flowering dogwood tree. Catherine had a tear running down her cheek as she stared through me.

Benjamin shouted like he was presenting a magicians act. "What do you think of my Heaven, Detective Reign? Isn't it grand?!"

"Heaven?" I said, putting Catherine out of my mind for a moment. "You call this Heaven?" I felt myself start to unhinge as the torment of the past few weeks freshened in my mind. "Heaven doesn't trap you in the middle of your worst memory or force feed you hearts as it tries to seduce you. Heaven doesn't attack you with hordes of crazed maniacs, or leave other ones to rot in the dark. For all I know the wine you're drinking is blood and the horses are diseased and dying."

Benjamin blew out a puff of smoke and smiled. "Still haven't figured it out, shame. It really is a marvelous work. I assure you that the wine here is quite delicious, and the horses are of the finest stock.

Well, quick witted might not be your strong suit, but allow me to express how impressed I am that you still have such spirit. You see this Victor," Benjamin shouted, tossing his wine glass against a rock. "This is how a man should handle his guilt."

"What did you do to them?" I asked slowly.

"Good question, Detective. I merely guided them on a path were they could find peace, here—as I want to do with you. One cannot enter the gates of heaven lest they be of pure heart. I am an advocate for one of the great powers, and I have brought them into the fold."

The way he was speaking, advocate for a greater power, *his* heaven, guilt, lest; it reminded of many years ago when Kelesa would read out loud when I was trying to sleep. *Scripture.*

"I know it's hard when the world has forgotten all about me," Benjamin said chuckling, "but I think you might have finally plucked at the right string."

My only answer made no sense to me, but I said it anyway. "You're... the devil."

"Indeed," Benjamin said excitedly as his cigar smoldered bright red. "I am one of them,"

I took a step back. "There's more than one?"

Benjamin nodded, and waved pleasantly at a passing carriage. "Iblis, Osiris, Mara, Vritra, Pan, Satan, we've all been waiting in the shadows, challenging mankind, tempting them, guiding them astray some might say. Our subtle touches brought many followers, but eventually subtly must give way to candor. When the time was ripe we built the Towers, each in our own vision, expressions of our passion for finding faithful followers by granting them extraordinary favors. Earlier you asked my name Detective, ask me again."

A surge of insignificance seemed to press down upon me as I stood there helpless and broken. At that moment I felt the raw power of the man standing before me and trembled. "Who are you?"

Benjamin pulled out his cigar and smothered it out on the backside of his hand without any expression. "My name is Lucifer. And you Detective have dragged yourself through purgatory, paradise, and hell to find *me* in Heaven. Congratulations."

Chapter 31

Like everyone else I knew the gist of Lucifer, but he was old superstition, on par with Zeus and Hades. A fallen angel, banished from God's presence, set to challenge God's will for the souls of men. Purgatory, paradise, heaven and hell were even more imaginary, but I felt my bubble burst as black feathers began littering the grass.

The black creatures in the sky began descending, and then the first angel flew over my shoulder, landing next to Lucifer while a dozen more dropped from the clouds like hungry ravens, their wings folding behind their backs as they landed. Dark beauty surrounded each of the men and women. They were dressed in their Sunday best, and despite their grave tone I saw genuine acceptance in their eyes.

"I don't believe you," I stammered.

"What do you believe in, Detective? Lucifer asked. "It was belief that killed your wife after all."

I felt my mind stretching to the limit as it tried to find solid ground, some place that made sense. "She was a threat to you then?"

"You've made quite the effort to destroy my work," Lucifer said calmly. "I've lost the Master of Mirrors, destroying my means of helping the outside world for a time. My daughters, Harlah and Loral's work has suffered, and you're the first person to make it out of Hell intact in a long time. But despite that, yes, your wife was a far greater threat. "

"Good for her," I said proudly.

Lucifer glared at me, the whites in his eyes turning black. "Do you have any idea how long it took for the human mind to refocus enough to place the towers? It had been so locked up on ancient traditions and customs that I could only whisper to the world, robbed of the opportunity to show them what I could offer. It's only been five years, and I've brought mankind to the point where acceptance of one another has never been higher in history. Crime rates are at an all time low, bigotry and persecution barely even exist. Disease, starvation, you name it, I've fixed it. People turned to the tower for guidance and direction when others spurned them for their choices. Even people like Victor are finding a place in society, accepted for who they are. And yet when I tried to grant Kelesa happiness, she rejected me, gave the credit to someone else. Kelesa never cared for the tower—she wasn't willing to let it into her life even when I gave her a gift. Kara was no different."

I felt the spark of anger that I'd lost reappear, and with it a twinge of lost confidence rekindled, I turned to Victor and Catherine. "Is it just me or does that sound hypocritical?"

I saw Victor's eyes twitch slightly, but Catherine actually lifted her head to look at me.

"Don't you want to know what I gave your wife?" Lucifer said as Catherine stared back at me. "What she was going to tell you at dinner the day she died?"

Again I could hear Kelesa's voice as Kara passed her the cell phone, picture it perfectly as they slid into the back of the cab. "What you think? Should we tell him now or when we get home?"

"I gave her the gift of life," Lucifer said proudly. "They were on their way back from the doctor's office with the news. I could sense their joy," his voice grew dark and dangerous, "but then they thanked *him*."

Suddenly, my vision blinked in and out with every beat of my bleeding heart. All the pain I'd felt losing Kelesa and Kara sprung up like a striking cobra, but it felt so much worse. I struggled to stand, tried to use my bound hands for balance as I toppled from side-to-side. My universe had no foundation; my whole being feeling as if it were being shattered like glass before being swept away piece by piece.

"It may seem hypocritical," the devils voice whispered, "but I gave Kelesa the highest honor, and she cast it aside, clinging to her old fashioned ideals and beliefs. There can be no progress without change."

"Kelesa was pregnant?" I said breathlessly. "No…no that's impossible."

I didn't notice I'd fallen until my shoulder hit the ground. I felt paralyzed—my insides chewed up and crushed into a ball of sorrow. All I could see was my murdered family playing out a scene that never happened; hugs and laughter, excitement that Kara would be an older sister, that Kelesa would be a mother.

Lucifer stepped forward and looked down at me curiously. "That would explain why you made it through Hell alone. It can't be perfect agony unless you know the whole truth."

"I don't know what you want," I moaned, "You said you taught people to accept each other, why couldn't you just accept her."

Frantically, Catherine ran to my side, trembling. "It wasn't from the Tower!" she wailed. "Jared, the names in the mirrors…he only knew they would happen, he didn't make them happen. I overheard the Master of Mirrors… he just made them think—"

"Well that was unexpected," Lucifer said chagrined as he slapped his hand over Catherine's mouth. Effortlessly he dragged her back to Victor. "A bit fresh from the operating table I suppose."

"Leave her alone," I cried out weakly.

Lucifer pressed his lips against Catherine's ear. "Do you want to see Aaron again?"

Catherine shook her head wildly; looking possessed as her eyes rolled to the back of her head, mumbling that she was sorry.

Awkwardly, I tried to push myself up. "Heaven," I spat. "I never believed in Heaven, but how can this even begin to classify. You threaten people with their kids, you have a psychiatric ward, and you make people suffer? If this was Heaven, Kelesa would be here."

"I agree," Lucifer said patiently, "I can give you happiness, Detective. I can even give you your family. All you have to do is being willingly to accept the truth."

"And what truth is that?"

"That you are already dead."

Chapter 32

Two of the angels hauled me to my feet. I shrugged them off, my irritation bandaging my grief momentarily. "I wish I was dead," I said heavily, "but I'm not. And if this is what I have to look forward to, let's keep it that way."

Lucifer motioned to the park. "Look around you. It's beautiful here—peaceful. I know you can't see it from here, but right now every person in the city has found their own happiness. This part of Heaven is how humanity would craft New York City if it could ever see beyond their personal differences. Imagine a normal business day where people are passionate about their work, the world benefiting from each labor. And then each day coming home to a reward, where there are no limitations to what you can choose. My paradise, while just an illusion before, comes to fruition here. It's easy to make people happy, Detective. Just give me a chance. Surrender to the truth."

"These realms are not for the living, Detective," Lucifer said, putting a hand on my shoulder. "Do you remember when we talked at your family's funeral, how I tried to convince you not to enter?"

"That was Ben, not you."

Lucifer looked disappointed. "So sure? Let me explain something to you. Death is rather simple really. It is a state of mind, or state of being. Your feelings, your choices, your beliefs, those you love or worship, each guide you to where you want to be. I have given shape to those places, manifested them within Saints Tower in order to channel and direct those whose state of being is hampered or held back. Take purgatory for instance: You call them vipers, but in truth they are regular people who are locked in their own minds, drifting from one memory to the next until they come to terms with themselves. They may mimic life—dressing for work and brushing their teeth—but they know they are living a lie. It's the reason they are so primal when they come in contact with others who aren't. Harlah helped relieve them of that, she gave them hope and encouragement. She was a siren of peace and tranquility. You would have become like the others in time—one cannot simply shove off what they feel is unconscionable—but instead you chose to cheat and steal others of the opportunity to progress, marking yourself as unredeemable. Your violent nature led to ruthless murder as you slaughtered the innocents you thought were monsters, trapping you in purgatory forever, like Victor. But again you cheated, killing my daughter to get what you wanted. Then there is poor Catherine. Did she ever tell you what she did for a living, Detective Reign?"

"She's a surgeon," I said dryly.

"Did she ever tell you what kind of surgeon?"

"No," I said slowly.

"Do you have any idea what you have done to this poor woman, leaving her hopeless and stuck in her past, staked into the one memory she could never let go of. Catherine was a Cesarean surgeon—she helped woman give birth to children. She'd never given much thought to why she went into the field,

~ 192 ~

until one day there were complications with the surgery and a mother lost her baby. It was hard on her, but the part that haunted her was that the mother had given the unborn child a name. That woman's action pressed upon the memory of when Catherine had been pregnant as a teenager. It stirred in her mind until she gave her own unborn child a name, Aaron. Giving that child an identity changed her life, made her feel ashamed and guilty. She is still stuck in that state of being because you pulled her through purgatory before she could come to terms with it. Then you took shortcuts through paradise where she could have learned to belong, share, and find peace in hard work and penance, sending her into a hell that could have instead been simple, painless, and inspiring—a place to face her fears straight on. You asked why I had a psychiatric ward in Heaven.—it's for those who are still not quite ready to be happy. It's for people like you three, and for those who you killed on your journey here."

Lucifer waited in silence for me to say something. I understood what he was saying; I just didn't want to believe it. "Why are you telling me this?"

"Because I can't help you unless you accept reality. You, just like Catherine, are locked in your past—tied down by guilt that you couldn't save all those people in the fire. Always convinced that you don't deserve happiness because of actions you've taken in the rollercoaster called life."

"I'm not dead," I said sharply.

Tell the Detective how you got here, Catherine. What's the last thing you remember?" I saw Catherine's shaking wane slightly as she glared at Lucifer wearily. "Go on, I promised that you could talk to him. I know how much you respect, Jared Reign. Here's your chance to help him."

Catherine wet her lips hesitantly. "I…I was with Blake on the beach…and he thought it would be fun to go swimming in the storm. It was fun for awhile, but then we heard the motor. Catherine chocked up, looking sick. "The boat didn't see us…"

"We really do need the ending," Lucifer said politely. "Calm down."

Tears began streaming down Catherine's cheeks as she tried to continue. "When…it…hit him, there was b…blood everywhere, I tried to carry him back to shore, but I couldn't. Then…then when I let him go he woke up and panicked. He grabbed my shoulders. I…I couldn't get away…I couldn't breathe…" She held her hand up to her throat like she was being choked, and looked up at me. "After that I saw you."

Lucifer turned back to me, a sympathetic look on his face. "You see detective. The tower is not for the living."

Look for the lie, look for the lie! My mind repeated over and over, desperate to find a hole to escape through. *You are not dead, neither is Catherine. He's just toying with you.*

"Then why did the vipers kill Blake?" I asked, feeling that there was a discrepancy hidden there. "Why did they attack me and Catherine if we were supposed to be there—supposed to get better?"

Lucifer sighed impatiently. "It was an accident, the voices felt threatened by Blake because of Catherine's thoughts. Being accidently drown left Catherine with a residual fear of Blake that the others picked up on. You on the other hand were attacked because you came with the intent to kill. Even the least lucid of humans will react to danger. It was in your heart when you killed yourself. I can explain things all day, Detective, but why waste time?"

"If I'm dead, who cares about time," I growled. I turned to Victor desperately. "Herse, you came through the door right?"

Victor was on his knees next to Catherine, mumbling incoherently under his breath as his eyes moved wildly beneath his lids. I wanted to kick the man for being so easily cowed. He'd been the only person I could rely on, and now he was useless. I scanned the ground around him for his backpack, anything that might have given me a bit of hope, but it wasn't there.

"Do you remember the day I spoke to you at your family's funeral?" Lucifer said.

"I remember when Ben talked to me, not you," I said defiantly.

Lucifer moved toward me, and reached behind my back. He loosened the straps of the straight jacket at first, but then I felt a tug at my jeans. A moment later he was holding my Glock out in front of me. "What about the days before the funeral? What about the night you held this to your head?"

I felt my mind replay the memory as he painted the picture. "A bottle of whiskey, a flickering TV screen in the dark lonely living room," Lucifer whispered in my ear. "—the fact that Kelesa and Kara wouldn't ever be coming back home playing around in your head like a child's music box. You had dedicated yourself to them, heart and soul, body and mind, but then you were left with nothing." I could feel the cool steel of the guns barrel against my temple as he continued. "It took awhile, something inside of you was afraid that Kelesa wouldn't approve of taking your own life. But by the third time you'd put the gun to your head, it was either then or never—peace or suffering. Even beneath the intoxication you still felt the dull grinding pain of loss, and without Kelesa, you probably would have done it sooner. The trigger felt hard, stiff like the safety was on, but you knew it wasn't." Lucifer slapped his hands together next to my ear. "The sharp crack as the gun powder ignited didn't even last a second. Tell me, Detective, isn't it suspicious how you don't remember what happened between that moment and when we spoke in the cemetery? Don't you find it just a bit convenient that the first person that agreed with you about the nature of my masterpiece was a criminal? There are no saints in Saints Tower, Detective Reign—only normal people with different problems."

I probably looked like a criminal without an alibi, wide eyed and frozen with no way out. I fought to ignore him, but an annoying hope for relief overshadowed my sense. Everything he said was true. I had held that gun to my head; I'd even had every single one of those thoughts. I'd already found out why my family was killed, and like most murder it was for self delusion. If I was truly dead, then I could be left in peace, I could let go of the confusion and suffering. Death explained the unexplainable, right… The only problem was that peace had never felt so far away.

"Just let me hear the words and I promise you I will show you your family," Lucifer said. "In Heaven everyone is given what they want. They are allowed to experience their passions, be consumed by the work they strove so hard to achieve in life. Each person here has gone through a journey similar to yours, searching for that one thing that defines them, that gives them purpose, and then they get it. No one judges, no one is left out, and now everyone has a purpose. You want to be a family man, I can give you that."

I felt the word 'yes' dance on my lips for a few moments; I honestly didn't see any harm in it. Seeing Kelesa and Kara alive, even if it wasn't real was better than any of this; but for the first time the pain in my heart sided with me. He should have never killed my family.

"No," I said, standing tall for the first time since arriving. The moment the word was said I felt memories flood back. They were blurry, probably from the alcohol, but they rang with truth. My Glock's trigger had felt stiff as I pulled it; maybe it was nerves, or maybe I way over did it with the whisky, but the phantom resistance was the only thing that kept me alive. I hadn't been paying much attention to the TV, but the news had come on at

~ 197 ~

some point, announcing Saints Towers new names. That was the moment I first decided to go in the tower, decided to uncover the truth and deliver justice. I left the house that night, left the gun behind, and slipped into hangovers and blackouts until the funeral.

Lucifer's face didn't look like Benjamin's anymore; it was far too sharp as a hidden fury surfaced.

"Beltin said there were two ways into the tower," I said, shaking free of the straight jacket. The cool autumn air welcoming my bare chest as it fell to the floor. "I walked in. You asked me what I believed in, well I believe in justice. Always have. You are a murderer, and worse than that you define everyone by one emotion, one habit, or one responsibility. People are many things, and to base your existence off any one thing is a horrible injustice. Why look forward to a Heaven when all you get is life's makeover?"

Lucifer's teeth never moved as he smiled and said, "It seems I'll just have to lock you in the ward until you can see the truth. I'll see you in a few years, Jared Reign."

Angels stepped up on either side of me and grabbed my arms. "Oh, I almost forgot," I said. "Linva sends her regards."

The angels were just about to fly away with me in tow when Lucifer's hand shot up in the air, halting my dismissal. "Linva," Lucifer spat. "That woman never ceases to amaze me. She always finds a foothold for my *brother* despite my best efforts."

Urgently Lucifer turned toward the angels, and growled. "Remove him from my Tower! Now."

I'd seen reactions like Lucifer's from hundreds of different criminals. It always happened when the criminal discovered you were carrying all the cards. I wasn't sure what those cards were, but I was going to use them. I'd been a cop my whole life; I'd brought hundreds of people to justice for the sake of the law. Earlier I'd given up on justice, but that was before I knew that the tower was more or less this man. "You seem scared," I said quickly. The words felt like needles on my tongue, but I forced them out. "Something in the way you tremble when you think of your brother I think. Is that who Kelesa thanked for our baby?"

I got the reaction I wanted, but I didn't think it would hurt so badly. Lucifer was in my face before I could even blink, his palm pressed against my chest, searing the skin beneath to black char. I went limp between the angels holding my arms, dangling like someone being dragged to the stockade. "I built this tower for my *Brother*. I wanted to show him how much he'd been forgotten. Humans fall in love so easily, all I had to do was give them gifts, welcome them in with open arms, and all of his work was pointless."

"So...you actually killed my family because of jealousy. Is that your defining trait?"

Lucifer slapped me across the face and hissed. "I care for my brother deeply, but he is wrong to suffer all the frailty of your kind while you focus on nothing but yourselves. That is why I built a Heaven you all deserve! Never speak of him again, or I will unleash agony upon you on a scale that doesn't exist anywhere else." Lucifer pointed to the charred skin on my chest. "You see this, you are mine. You don't deserve his love."

"That doesn't explain why you're scared," I coughed.

Lucifer pushed away from me, and looked toward the angels. "Our *Brother* seems to think that this man can destroy my Tower," Lucifer announced. "He warned me of a living soul that would be seeking redemption, a simple man that would seek justice for the loss of a loved one. Well here he is, and he is wrong again. Jared Reign is like all the others, unable to see beyond mortal existence, unable to believe in anything bigger than what is in front of them."

I never could say I had a light bulb click on inside my head, or had an epiphany that solved a case in the snap of a finger, but at that moment it felt like everything from the moment I set foot in the tower made perfect sense. I still dangled helplessly, but my mind connected pieces of the puzzle like I was in a reality TV fight for the million dollar prize. Linva's film about Kelesa had nothing to do with finding her killer. Linva's advice that all happiness could be found at the foot of a child's bed actually meant something, and even cutting out people's eyes to find a way through paradise pointed to the truth.

"It wasn't coincidence," I whispered as Lucifer was about to speak again.

Lucifer lifted my chin haughtily. "What was that?"

"It wasn't coincidence," I whispered again.

"What are you talking about?"

"You said it was coincidence that the first person that agreed with me about the tower was a criminal. It wasn't. You've got the wrong man, Lucifer. I was only the distraction. I never had a clue how to bring down your tower, but I know who did."

I lifted my head up enough to turn and look at Victor. He had one hand free from the straight jacket and was cutting at the other straps with one of the butcher knives from the adult horror dolls. He was also grinning back at me with glinting mischief in his eyes. "That was some good acting, Herse," I said. "I thought he'd broken you."

"Broken me?" Herse said indignantly. "You were the one about to spread your legs for the devil."

"That's not possible," Lucifer said. "Victor's a murderer."

"You made a mistake," I said, laughing tiredly. "I should have seen it immediately—the man I met in the pawn shop wasn't the same person I locked away years ago. That man would have gutted me like a fish. I should have seen it again when he spared the lives of the girls in the hotel. I thought it was because he knew I would have never agreed to go along with him it if he had killed them, but that wasn't it. Victor has always wanted people to embrace life, cherish each moment. The moments leading up to death always gave the people wasting their lives that thrill—the chance to cling to every last moment. Victor's is a smart man, brilliant in ways I can't even understand, but he never understood one thing.

When he met Amber he found it. I don't know the details, but death was probably a stupid answer after finding love. Then you took it away from him, killed her for giving away the fortune you supposedly granted her." Victor was still silently smiling from his knees as Lucifer eyes went wide. "I'd being willing to bet that he's been praying this whole time."

I remembered tucking Kara into bed at night; laughing and tickles were a nightly ritual, but so were the whispers I had to wait for before I could enter her room. Linva had been telling me what to look for; telling me how such a simple, child-like action, could be the start of redemption.

"Trust me," I said pulling myself up a little. "I wouldn't have seen it coming either. I would have been the last one to forgive Victor, and I would have been even farther in the line to think he'd ever feel sorry. Kelesa would have seen it though—she always told me it was never too late for anyone."

Lucifer shook with fear as the truth hit him. "No," he breathed. "No."

"You said the Tower cured bigotry and persecution, well Victor is not *just* a murder. Believing in people has never been my strong suit, but all you did was trick the world from having faith. Everything else was just them. It's always been there."

"You should get some sleep, Jared," Victor said as he freed himself of the straight-jacket. "You're starting to sound smart." He nodded at me with respect. "It was nice knowing you, Jared. I'd say we have about fifteen seconds left."

"Pleasure was mine," I said. And I actually meant it. "The look on his face is priceless."

Victor turned to Catherine and grinned. "What we do in life is only one side of the coin, Hun. Jared did right by you not letting the tower get its hooks in you. You'll be okay. Besides, red heads are the best."

Catherine nodded slowly and smiled.

Victor turned to the tower with his hands raised, and shouted. "And let the heavens crumble for the sake of our salvation!"

"There's that dramatic flair," I laughed crazed.

Lucifer was silent as Victor looked up at the tower, but he did point at his palm print on my chest. "You're mine, Jared Reign. You are mine!"

It took about twenty five seconds for the time bomb in Victor's backpack to explode. I wasn't sure how he rigged an alarm clock and all those wires to make such a large explosion, but the sight of the white stone falling on top of us and panicked angels who ran for their lives, was truly Victor Herse's greatest masterpiece.

The Last Chapter

I didn't expect to wake up. The experience of blood rushing through my veins as my heart beat feeling foreign to me. A ceiling fan twirled slowly above my head, the small wobble at its base giving me a sharp sense of déjà vu. I could hear voices coming from the next room, and I had to open and close my hands to make sure they were really there. I was on my back in a lightly lit hallway, the hardwood floor beneath me highly uncomfortable, but it was far preferable to being flattened like a pancake.

I rolled over and saw pictures of a families Disney vacation on the wall, and practically choked as I stood up. I was in my house, and by the flood of light coming from the living room window I would have guessed late evening. My body felt bruised as I stumbled into the living room where the TV had been left on. A bottle of whiskey was tipped on its side, dripping out onto the floor in a puddle. The room smelt like sweat and booze, but I didn't care. After what I'd seen, even the monstrosity of lost hopes and dreams was better.

I rubbed my head and plopped into the recliner. I was trying to sort things out, trying to understand why I wasn't dead, but new sensations kept distracting me. My hand reached for my chest, my fingers fumbling open the white buttoned shirt I was wearing and touching the scarred tissue of the handprint branded on my chest.

It hurt, and I felt my heart rate jump up to mach three as I remembered what it symbolized. Am I *still in the Saints Tower,* I thought. Maybe being a pancake wasn't that bad.

"People everywhere are still in awe after yesterday's tragedy," the news reporter on the TV announced loudly, catching my attention. I leaned forward in the chair as the camera flipped to a wide-angled view of Central Park. "Only three days after the Giving Mirrors shattered, injuring dozens, we all had to watch as Saints Tower suddenly collapsed. Many, including the Wise Ones, blame skeptics for the Towers destruction, but others are saying it's a sign of the end of days. Either way it has certainly left millions confused and panicked." The scene flickered to another Tower that was sandy brown. "However, concerns that the other towers have fallen worldwide have seemed to lessen as we continually get images and testimonials from other countries."

I found the remote and shut off the news as it went into how people were handling the tragic news. *If they had any idea what they were upset about*, I thought, feeling sick to my stomach. I sat up, wobbling from what felt like a massive hangover. Eyes squinted, I scanned the house, looking for any signs of, well, anything. Maybe the tower was broken, but maybe hearing the news was just part of the illusion.

I tensed with fear as the front door jingled with the sound of keys. I looked around the room and picked up the heavy whiskey bottle, holding it like a hammer. When the door opened, it smelt like caramel chocolate chip cookies and strawberry misted perfume all mixed together, and I felt my breath catch. I could feel the house come alive as Kelesa looked around the corner, looking at me like I was out of my mind.

"Mom," Kara's voice said as she tried to look around Kelesa, "What are doing? Get out of the way, please."

"Sorry," Kelesa said looking concerned. She took off her coat and hung it in the hallway before she walked into the living room. She crinkled her nose impatiently as she waited for me to explain myself. Slowly, I put down the whiskey bottle. I tried to speak several times before I realized I still needed to breathe. Kara was texting as she walked into the room, but quirked an eye at me and Kelesa curiously before retreating upstairs with a roll of her eyes.

I didn't say anything, I had no words. All I did was sprint across the room and wrap Kelesa in my arms. "Hey, I wanna know why you've been drinking in the middle of the day," she demanded, not hugging back. "I won't have this, Jared. Not in my house." She paused. "Are you crying?"

My laugh made her push me away, but when she saw the smile on my face, her hostility faded to amusement. "How drunk are you?"

I had five thousand things I wanted to say to her, but a million doubts that any of this was true.

"Bad day at work?" she asked, putting on her annoyed expression again. "I'll call Ben right now if I need to—"

"No!" I cried out, my fear making her flinch back. I threw my arms around her again, before she could escape.

"I heard you're pregnant. Is it true?" I whispered in her ear. My voice probably sounded like a wet squirrel had just been robbed, but I didn't care.

She opened her mouth, and then squeezed it shut in annoyance. "How did you find out? We wanted to surprise you." I felt my heart squeeze tight as it refused to let in any of joy it wanted so desperately to feel. "Is that why you were drinking?"

"No, no," I laughed. "I just… I just found out. It's amazing…" I said softly.

"Mom," Kara shouted as she ran down the stairs. "My friends are screwing with me. They say I've been gone for weeks. They are practically crying, well as much as you can in text form."

She handed Kelesa her phone. "Even my phone says it's a different day."

I looked at Kara wide eyed. "Kara can you give me and your mother a moment?"

"Did you hear what I—"

"I heard," I said. "Just a minute, please."

"Whatever," she said, sniffing as she walked up stairs. "Gah, you stink dad."

I turned back to my wife, who was starting to look worried. "Kelesa, can you tell me who Lucifer's brother is?"

"What's gotten in to you?" Kelesa said hesitantly. "It's like you've just found out the world is round. Of course I know who his brother is."

She told me, and I did know who he was, I just hadn't heard his name in a very long time. I knew seeing my family could all be an illusion—Lucifer had promised I could be with them after all. For all I knew I was just trapped in some psychiatric ward in Saints Tower, living out a fantasy. Part of me was tempted to be content, take this unbelievable phenomenon and run with it, but as always faith wasn't my strong suit.

I was Detective Jared Reign and knowing the truth was my job, even if it hurt. I wasn't sure if I could live with the consequence if I was wrong, losing my family again would be worse the death, but if there was one certainty I'd learned from Saints Tower, it was how to piss the devil off. Petrified, I fell to my knees as Kelesa turn on the news to an interview with the Wise Ones, and then closing my eyes, I gave Saints Tower's enemy all the credit, trying to ignore the burning palm print on my chest.

The End

www.ingramcontent.com/pod-product-compliance
Lightning Source LLC
Chambersburg PA
CBHW070830120626
46556CB00002B/700